MICHAEL HEATH

A Serpent's Egg

First published by Fara Press 2025

Copyright © 2025 by Michael Heath

All rights reserved. No part of this publication may be reproduced, stored or transmitted in any form or by any means, electronic, mechanical, photocopying, recording, scanning, or otherwise without written permission from the publisher. It is illegal to copy this book, post it to a website, or distribute it by any other means without permission.

This novel is entirely a work of fiction. The names, characters and incidents portrayed in it are the work of the author's imagination. Any resemblance to actual persons, living or dead, events or localities is entirely coincidental.

Michael Heath asserts the moral right to be identified as the author of this work.

First edition

This book was professionally typeset on Reedsy.
Find out more at reedsy.com

For Marian

The sister everyone should have.

And therefore think him as a serpent's
egg,
Which, hatch'd, would as his kind
grow mischievous,
And kill him in the shell.

WILLIAM SHAKESPEARE

JULIUS CAESAR

THE SHOCK OF THE OLD

"It wuz a white feather."

"Oh…" Winifred Smy laid down the iron as a gesture of respect, realising that Mrs Gladwell had alluded to something deeply significant.

"He wuz so hurt. To think that this sawny Becky Lummis woman, not much older than my youngest, should tayke it 'pon 'erself to shame the good men a' this parish who goo to war. And all the time our poor Billy wuz serven at the front. He wuz only 'ere cuz he's home on leave."

"War brings out the worst in people, doesn't it? I think there are many like our Miss Lummis who have no idea of the consequences of their actions."

"Well, I have no question 'gainst the girl's motives fer doing what she did. There are men enough of this parish that should be thinken 'ard 'bout their King and country at this very moment. But she should have taken the precaution to have checked with my Billy first afore insulting 'im like that."

"I can't agree, I'm afraid, Mrs Gladwell. Humiliating any man in public in an attempt to make him sign up is an appalling act in my opinion. I sometimes wonder how many men have been coerced to join up by a gesture such as that, only to die in some far-flung battlefield or ocean. And for what? Have these working men and their families ever profited from their sacrifice? I think not."

Mrs Gladwell's tongue rolled around the inside of both cheeks as she heard Miss Smy out, and her right shoulder stiffened in a barely discernible gesture of disagreement. "There we must disagree, Fred. And I don't tayke against yew very offen but on this occasion, I think yew very wrong. It's a brave act to put onesel' forrard to protect our way of loife. As yew well know, I've three sons in the Suffolks, and proud of 'em all."

"All I'm saying is let the choice be theirs and theirs alone. No bullying. No shaming. If someone makes the decision to place themselves in great danger for a cause they think deserves it, then it should not be influenced by those who remain in some safe place hundreds of miles away from the front line."

Smy wanted to pursue her argument but, seeing the fixed expression on Mrs Gladwell's face, decided that doing so would achieve nothing. She smoothed out the sleeve on the ironing board and took up her iron again.

"Well, that tea was lovely. Dew yew let me wash up these few things."

"No, you leave them there and I will do them as soon as I've finished this blouse."

"Oh, 'ave yew 'eard the news?"

Miss Smy placed down her iron once more. "Is it about the Balthasars? I thought that was all done with now."

"No, not the Balthasars, though that wuz an awful thing, wussent it? No, this news is now the talk of Fram. However, it does concern something rather disreputable. It's certainly not the sort a' thing that I would call suitable entertainment."

"You've lost me, Mrs Gladwell."

Mrs Gladwell placed her bag on the chair. "A moosic hall star, no less. But from what I've heard, 'e sings the sort a' songs and says the sort a' things that would have your good mother hooly turnen in her grave. I, for one, will not be present when 'e appears on any stage in this county, big London star or not."

"And coming to Framlingham? Well, that is news. Yes, I can imagine that if his act is *risqué* it may not appeal to you and a good many others besides. But having seen one or two myself…"

"Fred! When did yew see such things?"

"In London. There were hundreds of such places when I worked there. It was not my idea of entertainment either, but if you've never seen music hall acts for yourself, how can you pass judgement? Having said that, you might enjoy many of the other acts, the magicians and acrobats and so on, but you may need to close your ears to the words of one or two songs."

So surprised was Edith Gladwell by Smy's disturbing revelation, she promptly sat back down again, not even noticing that she had her now-crushed handbag underneath her. "Well, Fred, yew do surproise me. I would never ha' thought of yew attending something so…so ungodly. Yew've never mentioned that yew did such things afore."

Miss Smy folded up the ironed blouse and smiled patiently. "Oh, Mrs Gladwell, it was all rather chaste, really. I remember Marie Lloyd singing a song called…what was it now? Oh, something about taking a morning promenade. I don't pretend it was great poetry, but she had a way of singing and looking at the audience that implied much more than the words she was singing. A very talented woman, I thought."

"Hmm, mebbe so. No, my mind is hooly made up and when my mind is made up, it stays made up. So let's leave the matter there. Where's my bag gone?"

"You're sitting on it. Oh, don't get me wrong. I was against so much of what I heard, and thought that it still all rather came down to pathetic men leering in a knowing way at women, as too many men are wont to do. But I can't deny that some of the acts were performed with great skill. Some of the people are quite famous now. Not just Marie Lloyd, but Little Tich, George Tobey, Vesta Tilley…"

"Vesta Tilley? The one that dresses as a man? I can tell yew that there are a good many things that require great skill but that dussent mean that any decent mother would want 'er daughter to be doing so for a few greasy coppers. There's enough of them doing unspeakable things in Ipsidge at this very moment with great skill."

"But back to William. What has he told you about the war? How does he think it's going?"

Mrs Gladwell pressed her lips hard together and shook her head. "He dussent say anything about the war, which is very frustraten when 'e seems so 'eavily involved in it. Whenever I ask, 'e just changes the subject. Per'aps he's signed summat secret. Mebbe he's not allowed to talk about it."

"I saw him in Earl Soham last week and he seemed much quieter than usual. Very much taken up with his own thoughts. That's certainly not the William I used to know."

Mrs Gladwell didn't reply but seemed to fall into a reflection of her own. Smy regretted having turned the subject back to her son, having already heard that many who had returned on leave from the front were equally reluctant to communicate what they had seen. She therefore decided to switch subjects once more.

"Anyway, who is this great man? This bright star that's

honouring Framlingham with his presence. You haven't told me his name."

"Oh, summat Morrie. Now for the loife of me, I can't think what 'is first name was."

"Morrie? Was it Laurie Morrie?" asked Miss Smy in a strangely constrained voice.

"Thas it! Laurie…oh, Fred. Yew've gone all pale. Are yew all right?"

THE MISERABLES

The pain in Miss Smy's head was excruciating. Having not yet opened her eyes, she became slowly aware that - as she gained a vague consciousness - there was something very familiar and not familiar.

Within the tormented girdle of her skull, her thoughts were slowly arranging themselves into some degree of lucidity. What had she been doing? What was that awful pain that sat like a jagged stone pressing mercilessly into the back of her eye sockets?

Having realised that she was beginning to lose all feeling in her right arm, she now gently pulled it towards her, having become aware that it must have served as an improvised pillow during the night. As she manoeuvred her arm down, a splintering of glass immediately followed and she opened her eyes to see what she had done. On the unforgiving stone flags of her floor lay the shattered shards of a tumbler, sitting amongst specks of beer lit by sunlight coming in through her kitchen window.

Pulling herself into an upright position with the slow and painful discomfort of Gulliver pulling himself free of the Lilliputian chains, the world around her started to make sense. An almost empty flagon of ale was on the floor by her small wingback chair. A bottle of wine, its contents drained, stood disapprovingly on the kitchen table. She saw that she was still dressed, although her blouse and skirt exhibited all the signs that they had been her bedclothes for the night. A pile of neatly folded ironing - the very clothes she had been pressing the evening before when Mrs Gladwell had called - remained on the kitchen chair. She had intended to take the clothes upstairs and to put them into their respective drawers, but now she could see tell-tale brown drips on the last blouse she had ironed, testament to her unsteady pouring of the beer the night before.

Still the ache in her skull continued to throb as if a mailed fist was turning itself inside her head, slicing at the tissue and nerves, scoring deep lines of agony across the surfaces of her forehead and temples.

What had she been doing? What had driven her to break a promise she had made to herself so many years ago? The beer-spattered blouse that sat at the top of the ironing was the link to the conversation with Mrs Gladwell. From there the events of the previous evening arranged themselves soundlessly into one linear sequence. At first she couldn't remember Mrs Gladwell leaving, but some of the fog in her mind lifted to reveal the final words of reassurance to Mrs Gladwell that she had just 'had a turn' and would be fine. She thought that Mrs Gladwell, never one to want to make space in her mind for the tribulations of others, had probably been happy to take her leave.

Smy's left hand, as it drew back from her thigh, fell on an envelope with nothing but the word 'Win' upon it, written many years before by a neat slanting hand. She picked the envelope up and, noticing that it was empty, looked around for the letter that had always been kept within it. Feeling under her skirts with her other hand, she carefully pulled the two precious leaves of paper out, now crumpled and looking rather forlorn. She folded the letter, like a priest might fold the crisp linen cloth that had covered his altar, before returning it to the envelope and placing it on the arm of the chair.

Winifred Smy looked across the kitchen to where the kettle squatted, weighing up whether she had the necessary powers of coordination to make herself some tea. Her body, if it could have spoken to her, would have clearly communicated that to remain in the present position was its infinitely preferred option. Whilst staring at the kettle, her brain once more returned to the name Mrs Gladwell had casually told her. In that moment, the gates of an emotional lock were breached, and memories, feelings and hurt flooded through to stupefy her senses as her mind was flung back to one bitterly cold autumn in London many years ago.

Smy rubbed her hands across her eyes knowing that her cheeks were lined with dried-out streaks of tears. It even hurt when she tried to comfort herself by resting her hand across her forehead. Of all the discomfort that raddled her body, one awful sensation began to rise within her. Realising just what was happening, she rushed from her chair to the kitchen sink and was violently sick. Breathing hard and staring at the chips and pock marks of the stoneware sink, she heard to her dismay an enthusiastic knocking at her front door. Quietly, she crept upstairs and flung herself onto her bed and was soon asleep once more.

A SURPRISE INVITATION

Dear Miss Smy

I thought it best to introduce myself first as, even though we met many years ago you will, I am most certain, have long forgotten me. My name is Alfred Carver and I am the manager of the celebrated individual of the music hall, Mr Laurie Morrie. Of course, when we first knew each other, I was the dresser at The Paragon Music Hall. It was a modest occupation in - as you will recall - a very modest theatre, but it was a good and sound apprenticeship nonetheless for one such as myself.

Like many in this beautiful part of Suffolk in which you reside, you are probably already aware that Mr Laurie Morrie has been engaged to perform at the Assembly Hall in Framlingham on Friday the 23rd and Saturday the 24th April, as part of a fund-raising event for our brave men in uniform. Because you and Mr Morrie are long known to each other and, as he will be performing in a location that is so close to your own place of residence, he thought it would be the perfect opportunity to meet with you and to talk about the old days. He harbours - as indeed I do - nothing but the finest and most tender memories of you and, despite his unparalleled artistic reputation now, has never forgotten those days when he was a struggling performer and the lifelong friendships that were forged in those early times.

He expects to arrive in Framlingham on the morning of the first night of his performance and was wondering if you might be free to do him the greatest honour of joining him for lunch on the same day? Both he and I are staying at The Crown Hotel for two nights, a place which I'm sure you will know.

If you would be so kind as to send me your acceptance of this invitation, then I would be humbly grateful to you.

Your servant always

Alfred Carver

Smy put the letter down and stared at the tiles of her kitchen floor. "Lifelong friendships?" A twitch of cynicism could be fleetingly observed on Smy's face as she said the words. How long had it been, she wondered. She'd first moved to London in 1890, desperate to escape the limited future that a small Suffolk village offered. London had represented everything she had longed for: culture, music, and different varieties of excitement. But the reality of what she eventually found had cruelly exposed her naiveté.

"I did knock. Your door was wide open."

"Inspector!"

"No, you're supposed to call me Herbert. I thought we'd agreed that."

"Yes, yes, yes, when you're not on duty. But you surprised me."

"Can I come in?"

"You're already in. Sit down and I'll go and shut that front door. You never know what riff-raff will enter."

The Inspector put his hat on the table and sat wearily on a kitchen chair. "I called yesterday, as a matter of fact. About ten o'clock or so. You must have been out."

"Ah, so it was you," said Miss Smy, re-entering the room. "I was…not feeling very well. Taken myself to bed."

"Oh, sorry to hear you've been ill. Serious?"

Smy was beginning to regret the turn of conversation and shook her head. "It was nothing. Just a silly cold. Now, can I get you some tea?"

Tranmer watched Smy methodically arrange the crockery. He'd become used to the briskness of her movements, always as if she was slightly annoyed with whatever task was at hand. In fact, he realised, it was the manner of all her motions. She walked briskly, cycled briskly, even rode a horse at a bracing canter. As he continued to observe her, a barely perceptible sadness fell across his face.

"Cake?"

"Oh, no. Just tea would be perfect. Tell me, what was it that was playing on your mind when I entered? You looked to be in something of a reverie."

"It was nothing, just recalling a certain time in my life."

"Tell me about it. I'd love to know."

"It's not very interesting. In fact, tedious to the nth degree. Middle-aged people recounting their youth is something to be avoided at all costs, so don't expect me to share any such memories with you."

Smy realised that Carver's letter still lay open upon the kitchen table and she took the first opportunity to return it to its envelope.

"How have you been keeping, Herbert? Is the good constabulary of East Suffolk keeping you busy?"

"I'm not going to tell you."

Smy, now holding the tea tray, stopped in the middle of the kitchen having been taken aback by the brusqueness of

Tranmer's response. "Why are you not going to tell me?"

"Oh, because it's not very interesting. In fact, tedious to the nth degree."

Winifred Smy narrowed her eyes as a mock censure of the Inspector's response. "Look, I was thinking of something that was so long ago it has long since ceased to hold any relevance. But the events in your life are both recent and often have consequences. So don't start your verbal jousting with cheap tricks like that."

With the tea poured and both Smy and the Inspector relaxed in each other's company, they exchanged the gossip of Framlingham life. After a particularly prolonged silence, the Inspector looked uneasily at Smy. "Actually, there is something I wanted to tell you. Well, not only tell you but, well…to ask you what your thoughts were."

"You're intriguing me, Herbert. Out with it. Don't keep me waiting. What is this thing you want to tell me?"

"Well, since the Balthasars' case, we've hardly had a chance to catch up. And I…well, I've met someone. And…I think I am going to ask her to marry me."

"Oh!" Smy felt a sudden dullness balloon within her breast. She rallied and forced the feeling down. "Why, that's wonderful. I must meet her! Who is she?"

"Maud, her name's Maud Clemence. I met her about three months ago. Just before Christmas. She's the sister of one of the men I work with. She's a lovely woman and…well, I really like her."

"I am so pleased for you! You really do deserve to be happy again."

"Well, you know how I've been since losing Annie. And no one could ever replace her…"

"You can't think about Maud in that way. Maud's Maud and Annie was Annie. Anyway, I'm sure that Annie would have only wanted you to be happy."

The Inspector smiled boyishly. "You're right. But I wanted to ask you, am I doing the right thing? I'm not always so sure."

"Do you love her?"

"Love her? Yes, I think so. No, I'm sure I do. I'm just so mixed up and it's all been rather sudden."

Smy, unconvinced by Tranmer's response, chose to ignore it. "I'm sure you'll both be very happy together. And how can an old shrivelled stick of a woman like me deign to give you marital advice? I, the old maid-in-waiting."

But Tranmer didn't reply, instead he looked at her whilst a false smile appeared for a few moments and, as quickly, faded from his face.

When the Inspector had left and Miss Smy could drop the pretence of happiness for him, she walked through to her back garden feeling the need for some fresh air and the comfort of just being alone.

Aloneness or loneliness? Was it the latter that she now felt? How often had she resisted the advances of the Inspector and ignored the hints that he had trailed as he sought to find a way into her affections? But she knew she had been right to do so. People might talk of different kinds of love but Smy knew there was only one true form of love. Many years ago she had given someone that love and the memory of the calamitous events that swiftly followed haunted her still.

SCOTCHING RUMOURS

My Dear Mr Carver

You do yourself a disservice for I do very much remember you and those far-off days when we were all quite giddy in our youth. I have rarely met anyone who had such mastery of detail as you and I am sure that Mr Morrie (as I fear I must now call him) is most grateful to have in his employ a manager with such fine talents.

As for the kind invitation to meet with Mr Morrie for lunch, I must respectfully decline. Yes, I am flattered when you report of his 'finest and most tenderest memories' of me, but I am also certain that other memories will carry a taint that time will not heal.

I am certain that the show will be a great success and that those attending will be suitably impressed by the many fine acts that have been assembled for them.

Please do pass on my respects to Mr Morrie and enjoy your stay in Framlingham. Perhaps I might suggest that you and Mr Morrie take in a visit to the castle or the coast whilst you are in Suffolk?

Sincerely

Winfred Smy

Smy, standing in Debenham's Post Office reread the letter and, having decided that its contents were sufficient, placed it in an envelope and waited in the queue to buy some stamps. It was then that she noticed a poster on a side wall advertising the upcoming charity concert in Framlingham. Underneath the bold red lettering that announced the venue as the Assembly Hall, was the reassurance that over the two days there were performances 'At 7.00 pm on both evenings'. A picture of Laurie Morrie was accompanied by his sobriquet of 'The Cockney Sailor'. The image showed him looking upwards, perhaps singing the climactic notes of a tense love song, arms outstretched as if to embrace the object of his desire that appeared to be dropping out of the sky towards him.

Below Morrie's picture was a listing of other acts that ranged from 'Leonidas's Dogs' through to 'Marceline, the Mystical Mind Reader'. Smy smiled at the memory of similar acts she had first seen nine or ten years before the end of the last century.

"Will you be going, then?" So taken had Winifred Smy been by the poster that she had failed to notice that the queue of two people in front of her had dissipated. It was Molly Godbold, the postmistress, who had asked the question. She was a striking figure, not because of anything physically distinctive about her, but her appearance was, once seen, never forgotten. She wore the same clothes that she'd inherited from her mother and the sight of a late Victorian woman dealing with one's letters and other sundry purchases made many in Debenham feel as if they'd been flung back in time.

"I don't think so, Miss Godbold. Will you be going? It's sure to be packed to the rafters."

"I'd loike to. I 'ear he's quite a voice and a noice-looking man too, or maybe that picture there's a flattering one. They often are, yew know."

Miss Smy was just about to reply that, to her mind, the

picture would have been out of date by at least two decades, but fearing the conversation that would follow about how she could know this, she chose to keep her counsel.

"Just this one letter is it?"

"Yes, but I will take half a dozen stamps."

"Anything else I can do for yew?"

Smy laid the money on the counter and reassured Miss Molly Godbold that all her postal needs had been met. As she turned to leave, she was met with the sight of Nigel Manners' head pressed firmly against the outside of the glass door, his left hand shielding the sun's glare from his eyes whilst his right hand waved with a peculiar and over-enthusiastic speed.

As Smy gingerly opened the door outwards, Manners found himself awkwardly trapped behind it, being too slow to realise that he should have taken several steps backwards once Smy started to emerge.

"Just the woman! Just the woman I need to see! How are you, my dear Miss Smy? And have you heard the news? Your friend and mine to be wed! Dash it all, but Tranmer's a sly one. I had no idea that he was even in a relationship. And about time too. Last wife long buried. Time for the next wife to step into the breach."

Winifred Smy found herself constantly taken aback by the crassness of Manners' remarks and hoped, for Tranmer's sake, that he had not aired such an opinion in Tranmer's presence.

"It is indeed excellent news. Although I assume you expressed your congratulations to him in rather more considerate tones."

"What. Oh, yes, I'm sure I did. Soul of discretion, me. Always the right word for the delicate moment."

Smy was absolutely certain that he hadn't found the right

word for Tranmer's delicate moment. "Anyway, Mr Manners, you seemed to be looking for me? Don't tell me that you have a reputation to resurrect with your editor once more? I do remember our reuniting once over that very premise."

"Really? Me? My editor? Are you sure? Well, if it was, it's long escaped my memory now. No, I want to verify the most curious bit of tittle-tattle, as I'm sure that is exactly what it is. Something someone shared with me only yesterday. I am certain it is absolute poppycock, but we journalists must check our facts."

"Check your facts? Has the *Framlingham Weekly News* suddenly raised its integrity to new and unprecedented heights?"

"Oh, Miss Smy. That wounds me. Such remarks are not becoming of one of your standing. But I must forgive you and turn swiftly to the matter in hand; one must continue one's journalistic mission to separate pure truth from mere *bavardage*. It's regarding the eminent person who will soon be gracing Framlingham with his splendid presence, Mr Laurie Morrie."

For some reason known only to Manners he had removed his hat as he said this and placed it over his heart, much as he would have done if King George himself had just walked past in Debenham's High Street.

Miss Smy became instantly wary of Manners, something which he noticed immediately. "Ah, your reaction seems to answer my question."

"I find myself uninterested in your question, Mr Manners, so don't ask it."

"A Mr Carver has been in contact with our esteemed paper about publicity for the concert in Framlingham, and he claimed that you and Laurie Morrie were old friends. So you simply must tell me, did you and Mr Morrie..."

It had been raining hard that morning and the belly of the awning above Manners' head sagged with the rain that had gathered within it. With a deft movement of her umbrella, Smy sharply prodded the underside of the distended section which immediately engulfed Manners in a shower of water. She then wished him a good morning and walked on up towards the church.

Manners stood in the same position - hatless and with his body held in a stiff reverence - whilst the remaining water dripped from his thin face.

"...once know each other? And..." Manners sighed to himself, "...quite obviously, you did."

FOR OLD TIMES SAKE

"She'll be there. Why, I'd put good money on it. Airs and graces, that one. I could tell yew a few things about her I could, but the tellen of it would make my face glow with the shame of the tellen."

Smy laughed at the irritation of Gladys Cupper, to whom she'd just related her recent conversation with Edith Gladwell. "Well, she was quite adamant. The stars of the London music hall must get by without her patronage."

A metallic rap told Smy that there must be post but it was Mrs Cupper who went out into the hall to retrieve it. "Just a' one. Here yew are."

It was a long brown envelope addressed in handwriting she couldn't recognise. The stamp bore a London postmark and had been posted the previous day. "Do you mind?" Smy asked.

"Norra bit."

Smy took her paper knife and slit the envelope open. There were three items inside: two tickets and one short letter. The tickets, made of cream coloured card and almost square, were each headed 'Complimentary Free Pass' below which was the venue and date. Smy picked up and unfolded the letter, which had been hastily written.

Dearest Fred

Alf Carver tells me you aren't coming to either of the shows. But you must! Even if I have to walk to your puny little hamlet and carry you back here myself. So spare me the indignity of that and do me the honour of accepting these tickets and bringing a friend.

I have some good news and I want you to be the first to know!

For old times sake, do come.

Lawrence

Smy handed the letter to Gladys Cupper, who walked over to the window so that her poor eyesight could cope all the better. She suddenly looked up at Smy. "Lawrence?"

"That's his real name. Laurie Morrie was a stage name he invented. He's not even a real sailor. That's made up too."

"Oh!" Mrs Cupper looked a little crestfallen. "Is 'e even a real cockney?"

"Well, near enough. East London, if I remember right."

"So yew mix with the stars! How did yew get to know 'im?"

Smy walked over and took the letter from her friend. "Oh, it was so long ago, I can't remember. I haven't heard from him, or..." Smy faltered a little before she continued, "Must be over twenty years ago now. I'd forgotten all about him."

Winifred Smy smiled unconvincingly and, sensing that Mrs Cupper was too astute and too long a friend not to know that she was lying, made for the sink calling out behind her, "More tea, Glad?"

"Hmm? Oh, not for me. So, are yew goin'? I would love to go but who could I go with? My ol' man would never be sin dead in a theatre. It'd mean 'im missen out on a noight in the Crown."

Miss Smy looked fondly at Gladys Cupper whose face was

now pleading like the little girl she had once been, knowing she had the power to grant her wish.

"If you go with me, Glad, then I'll go. Have you ever seen a show like it?"

"Never. Bit of carol singen, thas about the only show I've sin."

"Then let's go. I will introduce you to the great man himself, if you like."

When Gladys Cupper left the house, it was as if she had suddenly learned of a substantial inheritance, so wide was the smile on her face. Smy returned to the kitchen table and read the letter once more. The same old Lawrence, she thought. He was insistent as ever, but it was an insistence that was borne of a controlling nature. He had always demanded that the world be arranged around him to his own liking, and could be deeply unpleasant when that same world failed to stand in the right place or didn't hit its mark. Smy wondered if he'd mellowed in the intervening years, or perhaps success had had the opposite effect and fashioned a monster. The ingredients were all there: the self-obsession, the irrefutable drive, the passion for perfection. Was his current success the product of the taming of his demons - or had that same success cruelly unleashed them?

As always, whenever troubled thoughts decided to wriggle furiously in their attempt to escape their cage, she resolved to do something physical and decided on a brisk walk across the fields to Occold. Taking down her three-quarter jacket and the same umbrella that had been her weapon of choice when confronted the day before by Manners' unctuous questions, she was soon following the long footpath that ran parallel to the Eye Road, making first for Bucks Green.

The pattern of the weather seemed to be identical to that of the day before. Early rain had given way to broad swathes of sunshine so that it was difficult to know how to dress; in the full glare of the sun, Smy would regret having brought her coat, but when the clouds gathered and their shadows slumped across the face of the land, it soon grew chilly in the shade.

As she walked along the path, noticing that the rosettes of cow parsley could be seen all along the bank waiting to launch their parasols of creamy umbels, she felt a gnawing ache of doubt about having decided to go to the show at Framlingham. What would they make of each other? Why, considering all that had gone between her and Lawrence Wright, would she be willing to meet him again? She turned the questions over in her mind but the answers always directed her back to the same conclusion: there was unfinished business between them. Maybe that's what it was for Wright too. Was that the real reason he was so keen to see her again?

Smy reached the now-disused cooling pond that lay beside the ill-fated railway line that had once been planned to run between Kenton and Debenham. When the finance for the venture drained away, it was abandoned along with the small bridges spanning the larger ditches and the large red-brick arch that would have taken the line across the Aspall Road. Two coots were gliding away from the pond edge, wary of what Winifred Smy's intentions might be. Smy strode on, determined to still make for Occold. Once again, the clouds gathered above her and she felt a keen lowering of the temperature around her. She smiled wryly that perhaps nature itself was sending a warning to her about Lawrence Wright, as if Smy was a protagonist in a cheap romantic novel.

MEETING MORRIE

"Well, what do you think, Gladys?"

Gladys Cupper couldn't answer at first, still staring in wide-eyed wonder at the now deserted stage. The musicians were carefully placing down their instruments and following the line of those in the audience who were heading towards an improvised bar. The lights directly above the stage area had been dimmed and two volunteer stagehands were sweeping the area ready for the first act that would follow the interval.

"I don't know 'ow she did it. I've never sin anythin' loike that afore. Why, it would be frightenen to speak with her. She would soon know everything about yew. In fact, it makes me shiver to think what she moight tell others about yew. Where does she get those powers from, Fred? Why, it's not Christian 'aving powers loike that."

"Oh, they're not powers, Glad. Don't get yourself het up. It's all manipulation, to make you think that she has control over you."

"Well, I dussent see how it can be manipulation. Not with her. Why, she knew everything about that poor wooman that she got up there. She even knew what she wuz thinken. Thas not manipulation, Fred."

It had been 'Marceline, the Mystical Mind Reader' that had

most captured the rapt attention of Gladys Cupper. There had already been several acts: jugglers, performing dogs, and a comedian whose saucy jokes had brought a *frisson* to the audience unsure whether to laugh or be outraged (they moved quickly from the latter to the former). But, despite such variety, there was something about 'Marceline' that continued to fascinate Mrs Cupper most of all. When Miss Smy now looked at Gladys, she wasn't sure whether to let the illusion persist or bring her back down to earth with how Marceline's act worked.

"Can she really see what yew're thinken, Fred?"

"Oh, Glad. It's just a trick they play on the audience. Think about the questions she was asking us all. They were things that would apply to everyone, but we like to believe that it only applies to us."

"What do you mean? When she had that poor wooman on the stage, she seemed to know all 'er secrets. Whatever she revealed about 'er, the wooman agreed."

"Of course she did, because she was only asking things that apply to all of us. What was her first question? Let me think. I know, she asked, 'You have a tendency to be critical of yourself'. Well, most people here tonight are going to say yes to that. Then she said, 'You have found it unwise to be frank to others'. Are you going to tell me that there's not a day that passes when you don't prefer to keep something to yourself? Years ago, when I went to a show in London, there was one act I remember who had a partner who chatted to people in the bar beforehand, pretending to be just another ordinary member of the audience. But when the so-called mind reader came on, they pretended to randomly choose a member of the audience and called them up on stage. And who do you think that member of the audience was? Only the same person that the mind-reader's partner had been interrogating in the bar before the show."

"But thas cheaten, Fred!"

"Well, I suppose all magic is cheating, but it's still entertaining. Trying to work out how they do it - that's the best part."

"Miss Smy?" So involved had Winifred Smy and Gladys Cupper become in their discussion that both had failed to recognise a tall man approaching them, immaculately dressed but with a somewhat undernourished physique. He had a high, smooth forehead and a rather tapered nose that seemed to draw attention to the receding chin beneath.

"Is it Mr Carver?"

"The very same."

"Why, I wouldn't have recognised you. You have acquired a rather stylish sense of dress since we last met."

Carver took this as a compliment and blushed a little. "It is very good to see you again. I am nothing but the conveyor of a request from someone who would be most grateful to speak with you for a few minutes. I think you know to whom I refer?"

"Only if I can bring my friend, Mr Carver. Otherwise, I prefer to remain in my seat."

"Oh, I believe the request was that you came alone but, well, let's not split hairs. I am sure that he would be happy to receive your friend as well."

How different Carver was from how she remembered him all those years ago in London. At that time his accent was the unvarnished patois of his upbringing in Spitalfields and, although the burr of that east London dialect was still there, it had been turned into something else altogether. She well recalled how Carver never pronounced any 'th' when he spoke, with 'three' becoming 'free' and 'another' always pronounced 'anuvver'. Obviously, Smy mused, he had spent the intervening years transforming himself from the unsophisticated theatre dresser into the smartly-attired, urbane figure he presented to her now.

Carver led the two women through a door to the left of the stage and along a small corridor that reeked of stale sweat and the dubious odours of the dog act, the canine yelps of which could be heard above the urgent voices of the stagehands and performers. Carver reached a dressing room door and, with his ear pressed against it, he knocked twice and then three times. Smy immediately recognised the signal and was instantly swept back in her mind to backstage at The Paragon Music Hall on London's Mile End Road. Any other combination of those short raps on the door told the person who occupied the dressing room that it wasn't Carver and therefore would not be answered.

"Come!"

Carver held the door open for Smy and Mrs Cupper. "Visitors, Mr Morrie. One of whom you will know, no doubt."

The occupant was facing a makeshift mirror, his face bearing the last few daubs of greasepaint, and he half-turned towards the two women now standing in the room.

"My god. My god, Miss Smy, it's been a long time." He wheeled around in his chair and stared at her. "Time has been kind to you. You hardly seem a day older since we were all together in…when was it now? 1890? 1891?"

Smy took in the shabbiness of the dressing room before replying, "You haven't changed either. You still lie through your teeth, Lawrence. And your taste in dressing rooms is as it ever was."

"Listen to her, Alfred! Just listen to her. The same old Winifred Smy. Sharp as a tack. Wicked as they come. Why didn't you accept my invitation to lunch? We have a lot to remember."

"Having a lot to remember is the very reason not to have accepted. This is Gladys Cupper, a good friend of mine." To Smy's astonishment, Gladys walked a few steps forward and curtsied. "An 'onour, Sir."

"Ha! You see that!" laughed Morrie. "She knows how to address the great Laurie Morrie. You, beautiful Madam, have brought the Suffolk sunshine into my day. Are you married?"

"Indeed I am, Sir. An' e's a good man too."

Morrie pretended to be disappointed and leaned forward towards Mrs Cupper. "Then you'll have to divorce him. Come back to London with me. You won't regret it, I promise you."

"No, I will not, koind Sir. Even if yew are famous. An' you're a wicked man for even thinken o' such a thing."

Smy sighed. "Still the same old tricks, Lawrence? I presume your mature years lie still before you."

He threw his head back and laughed, running his hands through his thick mop of hair having forgotten that his fingers were still covered in greasepaint. Then he became suddenly serious and looked Winifred Smy in the eye. "Well, are you going to ask me?"

"Ask you what?"

"Oh, come, come. She might have been my sister but she was your special friend, was she not? Have your good manners deserted you? Don't you want to know how Eleanor is?"

"What do you mean she 'might have been your sister'? Has something happened to her?"

"Dead, alas, but only to me. I assume Eleanor is out there thriving in her own way still. As far as I am concerned, I have no sister." Morrie reached over for a packet of cigarettes and a leather case which housed some matches and a match striker.

"Then there is no need for me to ask you about her and your question was entirely invalid. Come, Gladys. We don't want to miss the next act."

"But I'm the next act, Freddie. I am topping and tailing the second half. Schmaltz first and ribaldry last!"

"You were ever thus, Lawrence. I wish you luck."

Mrs Cupper, starstruck and now quite mute with admiration, curtsied once more and then followed Miss Smy out of the room. As they sat once again in the hall, Gladys admonished Smy. "Oh, Fred. Yew were very rude. And 'im such a man as 'e is. There was no call for it. Manners cost nothen."

"You don't know Lawrence Wright like I do, Glad. He has an abundance of talent perfectly matched by an abundance of frightful conceit."

"Well, 'e wuz perfectly charmin' to me, Fred. I do wonder about you sometimes. You're not shy of bein' a little uppity yoursel'."

Smy found herself riled by the encounter with the evening's star turn. She had hoped that the passage of years might have brought a change to Morrie's abrasive manner, but then she realised that the same vain hope could be applied to herself. And why didn't she ask him about Eleanor? But she then realised that there was no need; she knew perfectly well that he would not have known or cared.

SMY FINDS HERSELF CENTRE STAGE

The stage lights, which had been especially assembled for the evening's entertainment, were still dimmed but as Laurie Morrie walked on, they slowly lit up to throw a yellow glow across the stage. Clapping and cheering spontaneously erupted from the audience. The small band, drawn from the available musicians that lived within and without Framlingham, played the opening bars of a ballad that had been such an enormous success in London for Laurie Morrie: *Kensington Kate*.

Morrie, now dressed in a sailor's outfit that would not be recognised by any serving navy man, bowed several times before raising his arms to quieten the applause. Eventually the audience sat back on their chairs and the small orchestra, most of whom were fine players who regaled their local taverns' habitués with the sugar and vinegar of Suffolk's folk songs, repeated the introductory music. That wasn't to say that all of the musicianship was of the requisite standard: the trumpeter's notes were thin and insecure, and the man playing the snare drum seemed to be studiously avoiding the rhythm established by the conductor.

A lone violin then played a plangent melody that gave Morrie the right pitch for his introduction to the song. He suddenly assumed a forlorn stance and edged towards the front of the stage, singing in a theatrically pleading voice…

"I stand here before you, Judge, guilty as charged
  I'll make no excuses when sentence is passed
  But, please, I implore you to hear one short song
  Whose words will inform you that I meant no harm
  Why was I loitering by some big old bank door?
  Let me tell you dear Judge, just who the loiterin' was for
  For that someone who asked me to wait
  Was the girl of my dreams, my Kensington Kate."

The pianist played a rising figure that ended on the shrill notes at the top of her keyboard, musically signalling to the audience that the chorus would follow.

"From Fulham to Knightsbridge
  From Putney to Bow
  There's no one quite like her
  And I ought'er know
  She's pretty 'n' dainty
  My Kensington Katie
  But she tells me that I'll have to wait
  Wait for the date to get married to Kensington Kate
  Yes, wait for the date to get married to Kensington Kate"

Already, there were many in the audience who knew the chorus and lustily sang along, quite drowning out Laurie Morrie's vocal. Smy fondly remembered the music halls she visited in her youth, with the audiences made up of seamstresses, coalmen, dock labourers, milliners, costermongers and slop-workers; the misery of their hard lives suspended for those golden moments when a sentimental ballad would transport them to their own personal vision of 'Cockaigne'. And now, in this draughty hall in Framlingham, she was surrounded by farm hands, shepherds, office clerks, horsemen, blacksmiths, plaiters and labourers. Once again, the relentless grind of their trades was temporarily forgotten as they sang a ballad about a part of London they would probably never see, and a woman that had only ever existed in the composer's imagination.

After the first of Morrie's songs was over, it fell to the intervening acts to keep the attention of the audience who were now all impatient for the star performer to return for his final number. The troupe of jugglers returned and soon caught their attention, followed by a magician who flummoxed them with a mixture of coin and card trickery. The final act before Morrie's return was a strongman who played the role of David to a tall, muscular Goliath who had been recruited from a nearby brickworks the week before. The audience was astonished as the 'David' figure lifted the Goliath character above his head and proceeded to carry him around the hall.

The triumphant finale of his act was when a barbell, which he assured all present, "Weighed no less than 2240 lbs!" was placed on two barrels. He then invited members of the audience to come up on stage and try to lift it. Of course, even the most physically robust failed to move it from the barrels. Just as the strongman walked slowly behind the barbell, someone claiming to be his manager dramatically took to the stage and - at great length - gave a rousing endorsement of the strongman's past feats of endurance and strength. Once this rather windy speech had been completed, the strongman eyed the barbell for some seconds before lifting it arms' length above his head and holding it there, accompanied by gasps from the audience. Having returned the barbell to its barrels, the strongman left the stage to a rousing cheer.

Once the music that had sounded the departure of the strongman had subsided, an excited hum of conversation filled the hall as all eyes turned towards the side of the stage from which Laurie Morrie would emerge. Suddenly, the conductor's baton jerked up and a jerky waltz rhythm filled the hall, although the poor snare drummer was still meandering through the previous bar. Morrie jumped out onto the stage and, once more, the same train of events ensued: the riotous applause; the faux-modest acknowledgement of the audience's enthusiasm, and then the raised arms so that he could continue.

The volume of the jolly oom-pah-pah of the orchestra had lowered but, with the encouragement of the conductor's rising left hand, it sped up and swelled, preparing everyone for the opening recitative of the next number. This time, Morrie simulated a variety of hornpipe movements to convey that, unlike *Kensington Kate*, this was going to be a song with a nautical bent.

The single ping of a triangle halted the orchestral instruments, leaving a rolling piano to accompany the first lyrics. This time the words were spoken rather than sung, with a suggestion of the original melody reflected in the rise and fall of the lines.

"I'm just a jolly jack tar
　Who has lately run ashore
　An honest, upright matelot
　And honest to my core
　I love my good old mother

And would never bring her shame
Helpful, truthful, courteous
Should be my middle names

Then I saw a nice young miss
    Lying prostrate on the floor
    Who told me that she'd hurt her knee
    And it was proper sore
    To hear her cry in so much pain
    Why, my heart was rent in two
    So I knelt beside that wailing wench
    And said 'here's what to do'..."

With a sweep of his arm, Morrie invited the audience to join him in the rousing chorus.

"Raise your skirt a little bit
    And let me have a peek
    I promise not to speak
    Inspecting your physique
    Raise your skirt a little bit
    It's only little me
    You can always trust a sailor from the King's navy!"

The volume of the orchestra died away and Morrie eyed his audience with a theatrical disdain.

"Now I know what you're thinking
    And shame upon your soul
    She was at a disadvantage
    Lying there beside the road

But conscience and my honour
Was there upon that day
And that is why I with a heavy sigh
Felt so compelled to say..."

Once more, the audience skittered raucously through the chorus, enjoying the opportunity to savour the *double entendres* as if their lips had been coated with a forbidden meat...

"Raise your skirt a little bit
And let me have a peek
I promise not to speak
Inspecting your physique
Raise your skirt a little bit
My hands are warm you'll see
You can always trust a sailor from the King's navy!"

The song ended to tumultuous applause with the crowd demanding an encore, which was only satisfied when Morrie caroused the audience with one of the popular songs that had initially brought him to the attention of a wider audience, *Are Your Chickens Going Cheap, Mr Farmer?*

With the final encore completed and a visibly exhausted Laurie Morrie having finally left the stage, the bright lights of the Assembly Hall gave the signal to everyone that the magic spell had been broken and their normal lives awaited their return.

Just as Miss Smy was waiting whilst Mrs Cupper caught up with a friend she had failed to see in the audience earlier, Alfred Carver once more came into the hall looking to waylay Miss Smy. "Ah, there you are. Did you enjoy it? Wasn't he wonderful? He has a marvellous voice, hasn't he? You can see why he's so wonderfully popular now. And he's been so good to me, he really has. I love the man dearly. Oh, before I go, Lawrence asked if he could tell you some wonderful news. He said it won't take a moment. Just give him five minutes to move the last of his greasepaint, he said."

"Oh, can't he tell me all about it in a letter? Gladys and I need to get back to Kenton."

"I know what it is and, believe me, it's not the sort of thing you could trust to the post. It will only take a minute and then you're on your way. Now I must dash. I have to give a new contract to our strongman. He's quite the negotiator, I'm afraid."

"And a charlatan as well, Alfred."

Carver was taken aback. "What do you mean?"

"That barbell trick. I noticed that whilst the manager, or whoever he was, gave that bloated speech about his protégée's prowess, your so-called strongman was draining each of the two bells of sand into the barrels. That's why he was able to lift them and our Suffolk lads couldn't."

"Oh, Miss Smy. Why, you have got me there. For old time's sake, just keep that to yourself, will you?"

Smy smiled and, after Carver had disappeared once more, she waited some minutes before making her way to Laurie Morrie's dressing room, passing the small orchestra on the way. There was still a hubbub backstage, with various acts congratulating each other, or exchanging withering asides about the other acts' performances. Reaching the door, she gave the customary two and three raps on the door. But rather than hearing the answer 'come' as she had earlier, a single gunshot sounded clearly from within the dressing room.

Smy threw open the door and found Morrie slumped over his dressing table. It was at this moment that Smy felt someone push against her and now quite bewildered, she turned to see who it was, but in the commotion and panic they were soon lost in the crowd that had surged towards the door. It was the mind-reader, Marceline, who was the first to enter the room.

"What's happened, is he...is he..."

Other members of the various acts now filled the back of the small dressing room. A scream was heard by one of the assistants to the magician, who then immediately - albeit theatrically - fainted. Smy became aware that there was something not right about her coat and could feel an unfamiliar object in her right hand pocket. In her confusion she pulled it out and now held in her hand a revolver. And it was still warm.

SPARRING WITH SIBLEY

"Getting to be quite the regular, aren't you Miss Smy?"

"Not out of choice, I can assure you."

"First that poor butler last year in Grove Hall."

"Who, as was proven at the time, had not been murdered by me."

Sibley placed one hand on the back of Miss Smy's chair whilst the other gripped the table. Smy winced at the physical closeness of the Inspector, but kept her eyes firmly fixed on him.

"We do get all sorts in here. And I grant you, the poor butler probably wasn't killed by you."

"Probably? I'm sensing a degree of doubt still exists in your mind."

"But there's no getting out of it this time. So let's try again. Why did you shoot Mr Morrie? Spurned your advances? Perhaps you owed him money? Am I getting warm? I think I'm getting very warm, don't you?"

Smy pushed her chair back, forcing the Inspector to release his hold. There was something distinctly unpleasant about Sibley that Smy couldn't quite put her finger on. His small eyes reminded her of the weasels she would occasionally see scampering across Bellwell Lane, and the bulge of his stomach hung over a belt that struggled to bring the two sides of his trousers' waistband together. And then there was the bizarre habit he had of pulling an old handkerchief out of one pocket and inspecting it before passing it into the opposite pocket.

"I've said it before and I will repeat it only one more time for you: I did not kill Lawrence Wright, or Laurie Morrie, or whatever you would like to call him. I had no reason to kill him. I have explained to you what happened and am rather past caring whether you believe me or not. Charge me if you want to, but you will make an error that the senior officers in the East Suffolk Constabulary might not find easy to forget."

Sibley walked over to the wall and hitched up his trousers before looking out of the single high window of the interview room. He could just make out the three stars that made up Orion's belt. Smy took the opportunity to relax her demeanour a little, beginning to feel the tiredness in her limbs.

"Do you intend to ask me any other questions? I assume that you are not able to release me?"

"Release you?" Sibley wheeled around with a lightness that even surprised Smy. "Have you lost your senses? You're here because a man is dead and you were holding the gun that killed him."

"How do you know it was the gun that killed him?"

"Well, of course it was! People saw you with it and you were alone in the room when they entered."

"People saw me with a revolver, which someone had dropped fortuitously into my pocket. I have never carried a gun and certainly would never do so. If I had intended to kill someone I would not do it in a way that would be so obvious. I have been framed by someone for a reason I do not know and keeping me in this room has given the real murderer every opportunity to make their escape. All because you, Inspector Sibley, are concentrating your futile efforts on the wrong person. And now I'd like some water, please."

Sibley sighed, but nevertheless asked one of the officers outside the room to bring in some water for Miss Smy, which was set down on the table before her. She sipped the water and, when she was just about to place the glass tumbler back on the table again, froze in an attitude of thought. She turned to the Inspector and asked, "Has the body been identified yet?"

"Of course." It was now Sibley's turn to feel tired and he slowly rubbed the back of his neck and yawned.

"And who identified him?"

"Who? Oh, the music chap, Sterling."

"I take it you mean the conductor? I think his name is Spurling."

"Yes, Sterling, Spurling…what does it matter?"

Smy held the glass up and looked carefully at it. "Well, of course getting minor details right like someone's name shouldn't be important to a major police enquiry. Did you manage to look at the body before they took it away?"

He leaned back against the wall and nodded that he had.

"If I remember right, the body of Morrie was slumped forward face down on the table."

Sibley smirked, "You should know."

"And what about his hands, where were they?"

"His hands? One hanging down and the other on the table."

"If I can be a little bit more detailed than that, his left hand was hanging down and his right hand was still holding a glass, a glass not dissimilar to this one."

"I'm sorry, Miss Smy but I think it's time we called it a day… or a night, that is."

"Please, Inspector, do me one last favour and I will go meekly to my cell."

Sibley rubbed his eyes and yawned. "Is the favour a quick one, 'cos I'm not in the mood for this any more, Miss Smy."

"Do you have the murder weapon?"

Sibley was taken aback by the request. "The murder weapon? Of course."

Smy, in a newfound enthusiasm, quickly rose from the table. "Could you let me see it? I won't be longer than 30 seconds and then you will be through for the night."

Once more, Sibley trudged wearily over to the door and, following another brief conversation, the officer returned and placed the gun on the table. Smy leaned over and closely scrutinised it.

"Thank you, Inspector. You can release me now."

"Release you? Release you where? The only place you'll be released to is a cell."

"Do you recognise this revolver?"

"What do you mean, recognise it? It's a gun, that's what it is."

"The maker?"

Sibley glanced down quickly, before replying, "Webley. Webley revolver."

"And which version of the Webley is the revolver, Inspector?"

Sibley looked again. "Well, it's not a mark V. It's the one before. The mark IV or whatever."

"Wrong, Inspector, quite wrong. It's a Webley Mark VI service revolver. Considering that it is Webley's latest revolver and was only exclusively issued to the British army in the last few weeks, how would I have got hold of one?"

"Well, you seem to know enough about guns, so you obviously got it from somewhere."

"Then that is something you will have to prove. You will have to find out how a humble Suffolk spinster managed to purloin a gun of this quality and exclusivity. However, I think if you train your efforts instead on the origin of this handgun, bearing in mind that there will be many officers in England on leave from the front, then that might furnish you with a more successful line of enquiry."

"Don't think for one moment that's going to frustrate me. You have friends enough I'm sure, and anyone might have lent you that gun."

"Again, that is for you to prove and you will not be able to do so, I can assure you. And then there is one other thing. What liquid was in the tumbler when you found Mr Morrie?"

"Liquid? Errr…it was whisky or something. I'm not sure. Anyway, what do I care what was in the tumbler?"

"It might be nothing of course, but I can assure you that I find it very strange that the deceased should be gripping a glass of whatever it was that night. You see, Mr Morrie had many faults, gambling certainly, but not drinking. When I knew him, Mr Morrie had never touched a drop of alcohol in his entire life. All alcohol made him violently ill. I think it's you who have questions that need answering, Inspector, not me."

MORNING MANNERS

"Did yew sleep, Miss?"

Smy looked up from the makeshift bed, a thin blanket covering her still fully-clothed figure. "Do I look like I slept?"

The sergeant put a cup of tea on an adjacent chair. "Dew yew drink that. Yew'll feel a lot better 'bout things."

She wearily swung her legs around and sat on the edge of the bed. "What happens now, Sergeant?"

"Oh, I carn't say much, but I 'eard that the Inspector seemed a little crushed last night. 'Ad to go see a body all of a sudden."

Smy stretched her arms wide before rubbing the sleep from her eyes. "Well, I suppose it won't change anything very much. Whether it's Morrie or someone else, they'll still think I shot them. Tell me, is Inspector Tranmer in?"

"He is."

"Can I speak with him?"

"'Fraid not, Miss."

Smy looked surprised. "Why ever not?"

But the sergeant smiled rather enigmatically and left Miss Smy to enjoy the questionable comforts of her Framlingham police cell.

She stood up and adjusted her clothing. Smy felt grubby and, somehow, this made her feel all the more anxious. She sipped a little of the tea but its sweetness made her wince, so she quickly returned it to the chair. The cell was cold and a shrill April sun was just visible through a small window that was tucked into the meeting point of the wall and roof. It was as she was gathering her thoughts that the jingling of keys outside indicated that she should prepare for another visit. She found her heart was beating faster, perhaps due to some desperate surge of hope, as the cell door was tantalisingly opened. Smy's hopes rose in anticipation.

Nigel Manners walked breezily in. Smy's hopes collapsed.

"Chin up, Miss Smy! Help is at hand!"

Smy sat down on the chair forgetting that the teacup was still on it and soon both cup and contents were in a sorry disarray across the floor. The sergeant, who had let Manners into the room, rolled his eyes and left them whilst he went searching for a mop, dustpan and brush.

Smy had found that all words failed her. In this hour of quiet despair, the obsequious, self-obsessed Manners was the last person she wanted to see. Manners, though, was utterly unaware of Smy's emotional state and took a moment to look around the cramped cell. "Well, it certainly ain't The Ritz, is it?"

"Why have you come here, Mr Manners? I do hope that it's not in a professional capacity."

Manners jerked his head back in surprise. "Professional capacity? Oh, Miss Smy, give me some credit, do. Even though our last encounter was ended by, shall we say, a damp conclusion, I bear no ill will. May one sit here?"

"If one must."

Manners inspected the rude bed, swept away some imaginary specks and lowered his skeletal limbs onto it. "Golly, a bit firmer than one might expect. Did you manage to sleep on this thing?"

Smy shook her head.

"Not surprised, dear girl."

"What did you call me?"

"Why…ah, yes. Maybe not 'dear girl'."

Smy buried her head in her hands and asked in a now muffled voice, "Again, Mr Manners, why have you come here?"

"Because you're innocent. That's why I'm here."

Smy slowly raised her head and looked incredulously at Manners. "You think I am innocent?"

"Of course! By the way, he was rather good, wasn't he?"

"Who?"

"That Morrie chap. I've been humming *Kensington Kate* ever since last night. Marvellous tune, don't you think?"

"You were there?"

"Of course. I managed to persuade my editor that the Framlingham charity bash was infinitely more entertaining than some monumentally heavy drama by yet another depressed Russian playwright. Wouldn't have missed last night for the world."

Smy swept her hair back and tried to focus her thoughts. For some reason that she couldn't quite determine, she was strangely pleased that she now knew that Manners had been present the previous evening, although she couldn't decide why this might be of any advantage to her.

"So what do you remember from last night? What's your version of it all?" Smy asked.

"Very little to say, really. I was chatting with my most beloved when there was the quite unmistakable sound of a gunshot. Even though we were at the back of the hall and it was still quite busy, I heard the shot nonetheless."

"And then?"

"Well, a frightful to-do there was. At first, people just looked at each other, and then there was a commotion near the door by the stage. By the time I got to the dressing room, that strongman and some other person had hold of your arms and were putting you in some dressing room for safekeeping. Shame about old Morrie, though. Jolly decent voice and everything."

"How do you know it was Morrie who'd been shot?"

Manners was taken aback by the question. "How do I know? Well…because I asked. This slip of a thing was walking past me and she told me that Morrie had been shot in the back at his dressing table."

"Mr Manners, you didn't answer my earlier question. Why do you think I'm innocent?"

"Didn't I? Well, because you are the smartest girl…err, woman I've ever met. You've helped me unravel some quite tricky murders, and I just can't believe that a person so mentally astute would kill someone in such an obvious way."

"I helped you unravel..?"

Manners held up a hand and superciliously closed his eyes. "If you would permit me to continue. As I was saying, from where myself and the future Mrs Manners were sitting, I was watching you talk to some theatre chappie and you just seemed to be entirely your normal self. No, it don't add up. It don't add up at all. I just can't believe that this completely composed woman idly whiled away the time after the concert, chatting to all and sundry, before shuffling away to some man's dressing room to pack him off to a better place."

"Mr Manners, putting aside the fact that it was my analytical skills that raised your suspicions rather than the integrity of my character, I am so glad that I have one person at least who thinks I am innocent. I can tell you, this is all a nightmare. And all I have are two lifelines. And even those aren't proof enough."

"Lifelines? What lifelines?"

Smy let out a long sigh and looked away to the one small window. "The first is about the gun that was dropped into my coat pocket by someone when I had entered the dressing room. It's a Webley revolver, but has only been recently issued to officers fighting on the Western Front. It's not much, but where would I find such a thing in my quiet life?"

"But how do you know so much about guns?"

Smy seemed uncomfortable with Manners' question. "Well, I won't reveal the origin of my interest, but my uncle - my father's brother - works for Tilney's in Beccles. He keeps me up to date with all that's new."

"What? Tilney's the gunsmiths?"

Smy laughed, "I'm afraid his enthusiasm is rather wearing. The last time I stayed with him, he insisted on showing me around the entire shop. I felt like I'd seen every firearm on the planet. Nevertheless, I thank god he's a Webley man or else I would never have spotted the fact that the distribution of the gun that was used was so restricted."

Manners resignedly shook his head. "Be that as it may, it's not going to..."

"It's not going to be enough, I know. And then there is...tell me, Mr Manners. Where would they have taken the body?"

"The body? I don't know, but it won't take me long to find out."

But the sound of keys being manipulated on the other side

of the cell door interrupted the conversation of Manners and Smy, and once again it was swung open. This time it wasn't only the stocky sergeant who entered, but the unmistakable figure of Inspector Sibley who was following close behind. He nodded as a matter of forced politeness towards Manners. "Short on scandal? I do hope you're not extracting information that would prejudice this investigation."

"Merely a social call. Fret not, dear Inspector."

But Sibley was now looking at Smy. "You were right. It wasn't Morrie you killed. It was someone else. And I'd like you to tell us who he was."

THE MAN IN THE MORGUE

Winifred Smy sat down with a triumphant smile on her face. Sibley looked unimpressed, thinking that it was an act of bravado to unhitch herself from the accusation of murder.

"My good Mr Manners, would you tell the Inspector what you have just told me."

Manners looked momentarily confused and one scrawny hand rubbed one greasy scalp. "What I told you. Erm…I can't think what I did tell you. Give me a clue."

Sibley, now irritated, quickly cut in. "Excuse me, Miss Smy, but I have requested that you come with me, right now, to identify this body. Mr Manners can save his answer until later."

"Oh no, Inspector. You have a body and I imagine that it will still be in the morgue at whichever time we look at it. I will go with you, but when I do so, I would like to return to my home immediately afterwards."

"Return home? What do you think we are? A boarding house or something? You will accompany me to the morgue and then return to this cell. After that you will be escorted to Ipswich where you will remain until your trial."

Smy leant back with an insouciance that raised the Inspector's temperature even more. "Escorted? Do you not trust me to find Ipswich Police Station myself? I've grown quite capable of late."

"Stand up, Smy! I've had just about enough of this. Stand up now and follow me."

Smy kept her eyes fixed on those of Sibley's. "I have one reasonable request, which can only be granted with the assistance of Mr Manners. It will take no more than a minute and might even change your mind about whether I am the murderer or not."

Sibley stamped his foot in anger. "Then do your worst and let us get on!"

Smy bowed her head in mock appreciation of the Inspector's acquiescence. "Mr Manners, you said that after you heard the gunshot you then went immediately to the area outside the dressing room."

Manners nodded, still nonplussed where the conversation might be leading.

"You then said that someone - a 'slip of a thing' I think you called her - answered your question as to what had just happened."

"Oh yes, her. The one that told me that someone had killed Morrie. That's right."

"And what else did she tell you?"

"Oh, I think that was all. Oh wait, that Morrie had been shot in the back."

Smy stood up and walked slowly towards Sibley. "Shot in the back. Now, Inspector, I would like to ask you a question. Where was Morrie's dressing table in relation to the door? No need to answer, I know you are fully aware that when one opens the door, the dressing table is side-on to it. Which then raises another question, of course. How could I, in the very short time between the sound of the gunshot and people bursting into the room immediately after me, have walked behind him, shot him and then returned to stand just inside the door?"

"Why not? You could easily have walked the few paces back to where we found you. Anyway, all I know is that you were the only person in that room when he was shot. How you did it is something we'll find out soon enough."

"Let's be clear about this, Inspector. You're proposing that I walked in and, even though it would be as plain as day that it was not Laurie Morrie sitting there, I would then walk behind someone I didn't know, shoot him in the back and then calmly pocket the gun and wait for people to find me? Is that really a plausible explanation to you?"

Sibley flinched and reached for his handkerchief, wiped his nose and placed it back in the opposite pocket. The tension was broken by a knock on the door. A constable entered, asking, "Sir, could I have a word?"

"Not now, constable!"

But the policeman, after looking around at the group who were assembled, lowered his voice, "I think you might want to see this, Sir. Believe me, I wouldn't trouble you otherwise."

Sibley turned his head and, with his temper still seething, looked around at the constable who handed him an envelope.

"What is this?"

"A statement, Sir. You asked us to take statements from everyone who was in the vicinity of the shooting.

"And?"

"Well, this lady who gave me the statement says that she was putting away some props or something and saw Miss Smy that night."

"Constable, can't this wait? A lot of people would have seen Miss Smy. That's because she was also, as you say, 'in the vicinity'."

But the constable was insistent. "Well, be that as it may, Sir, this lady was adamant that she saw Miss Smy knocking at the door just before she heard the gunshot."

Sibley snatched the envelope, tore it open, and quickly took in the statement. He then slammed the statement against the chest of the constable. "Take it away."

"But, Sir…"

"Take it away, I told you!"

The constable looked rather sheepish as he left the room. Smy said nothing and waited to see what the Inspector might say next, but Sibley walked to a corner of the room and looked at the floor. Winfred Smy could wait no longer. "It rather looks like you have the wrong person, Inspector. All the time that you have spent on me has given the real murderer valuable time to cover their tracks. I think I am owed an apology."

Sibley ignored Smy and turned to the sergeant. "Will you accompany me and Miss Smy to the Morgue please? Let's get this over with."

"May I come also, Inspector?"

"No, Mr Manners, you may not. I will let you know if we have made any progress in my own good time."

The morgue in Framlingham was a small building at the edge of the town and, after a brisk ten-minute walk, all three were assembled around the body which was covered with a heavy white sheet. A single oil lamp gave the cold room a sinister glow. Sibley motioned to the sergeant to fold down the top of the sheet and Smy leant over the corpse, carefully studying the features of the dead man, his pale skin catching the flickers of light given off by the lamp.

"Well?" asked Sibley, trying to muster as little enthusiasm as possible.

"Well, what?" replied Smy, teasingly.

"You know 'well, what'. Do you recognise him?"

"Yes, I recognise him."

"His name?"

"I don't know what his name is, but I can tell you that he was the worst exponent of the snare drum that I have ever heard."

Sibley first looked confused at Smy and then scrutinised the corpse as if the answer to the riddle lay there. "Snare drum?"

"I need to go now, Inspector. I assume that the charges will be immediately dropped? I have friends in Framlingham who I am hoping will take me back to Kenton."

As Smy went to walk away, Sibley half-ran around her to block her exit. "What is this about the snare drum? That's all I want to know."

Smy smiled mischievously. "I know no more than you do about that poor man. Other than what I have told you, I had never seen this man before last night. He was part of the group that had been assembled for the concert. His playing - if you could call it that - was awful. You have far better resources to establish his identity than I have."

Smy was glad to have left the morgue and stopped for a moment to breathe in the clean air. She was just about to make for her friends' house when the Inspector called from behind. "If this was an attempt to frame you, then there is someone out there who would like to see you hang."

"It wasn't so very long ago that that person was you, Inspector Sibley."

A CURIOUS SMELL

Winifred Smy decided that her friends' house was best gained by cutting through the grounds of Framlingham Castle. A steep path ran down on one side of the Castle Inn and joined a track that encircled the lake known to everyone as 'the mere'. Smy, still emotionally shaken by the events of the last thirty-six hours, found that an unrelenting onslaught of thoughts went careening through her brain. Certain events could easily be connected, but others struck her as decidedly odd.

Without doubt, the overriding sense that she found herself experiencing was one of enormous relief. Despite the bravado that she had mustered in the presence of Inspector Sibley, she'd been genuinely worried about the circumstantial evidence that was being put before her.

She tried to assuage her inner turmoil by turning her attention to the scene around her as she walked towards New Road. Long-limbed meadow buttercups were idly swaying to the rhythms of the lazy winds passing through. Orange-tip butterflies zig-zagged across Smy's path, as if daring her to try and reach out to catch them. A kestrel snapped the invisible string that it seemed to be hanging by before flying across the marshy grassland to hover anew.

Smy felt both dishevelled and tired, and so it was with

deep dismay that she saw Herbert Tranmer who was walking towards her. If it had been anyone else, she might well have turned and walked around the mere the opposite way, but realising that Tranmer might be a useful person to talk to, she pressed on.

Tranmer had, in fact, not noticed her at first as he seemed so lost in his own thoughts. When he realised that it was Miss Smy, he became a little flustered. Try as he might to adopt a posture that might conceal his discomfort, it was easily evident to Smy nonetheless.

He raised his hat and gave a slight bow of the head. "Good morning, Miss Smy. You appear to have, err…escaped. Have they dropped the charges?"

"I would think you already know the answer to that. Tell me, why wouldn't they let you speak to me? I specifically requested a meeting but they were quite unwilling to let me see you."

"Well, I think they might be worried that you and I are a little too…known to each other. I hope that you weren't too uncomfortable in the station. The cells are a bit draughty."

Smy picked up a corner of her skirt and raised her eyebrows to show just how creased her appearance was. "One may have found the opportunity to wash welcoming but, as you already know, I am not unfamiliar with the accommodation afforded by his majesty's pleasure."

"Are you heading anywhere in particular?"

"The Symonds are old friends of mine and I was hoping to avail myself of their hospitality. That's why I was heading for New Road. If I can just freshen up a little and eat something that's decent, then I can walk on to Kenton."

"Perhaps I might join you? I'm not in any particular rush."

Smy looked archly at Tranmer. "Oh, so it is not for the

pleasure of my company that you would walk a little way with me, but because you have nothing better to do?"

Tranmer put his hat firmly back on his head, smiled and with a small theatrical wave of the hand, beckoned Miss Smy to lead on.

"So, Herbert, who will be your chief suspect now that I appear to have been exonerated?"

"I've no idea. It has been stressed to me in no uncertain terms that the case is Sibley's and I must keep my distance. From what I have heard though, it's all rather baffling."

Smy nodded. "Baffling indeed. I suppose you know I was already acquainted with the famous Laurie Morrie? At least Gladys Cupper was delighted to have met him."

"Can I ask you how you know him? Manners rather thinks an awful lot of him. I never knew that you mixed with such exalted company."

"Exalted? Morrie is certainly not that. He was always a devious individual and I would give my eye teeth to know where he is right now."

"Sibley told me that you were found with the gun in your hand. Was that so?"

"Most definitely not so. I was found with the gun in my pocket. When I opened the door, I wasn't even aware that there was a woman already in the room. She was the one who had fired the shot, planted the gun on me and then fled the room in all the confusion. So, naturally, the people who then entered afterwards assumed I was the killer."

Tranmer stopped and dragged his hand through the leaves of a large willow, its branches curving gracefully to the ground like the many paths of a shower of arrows. "So what can you remember about this woman, the one that you say escaped?"

"Nothing. I can remember nothing about her other than a curious smell. Of course, the shock of the scene before me was so distracting that I was entirely unaware that the gun had been secreted in my pocket. She was quite the expert."

"You can't recall anything? Not even height, or how old she was, perhaps? Just a 'curious smell'? That's not like you. Your powers of observation are usually excellent."

"In moments of calm, I would agree with you, but on that evening too much happened at too great a speed."

They walked on through a small group of cows that tramped sluggishly through the meadow grasses.

"Petite." Smy suddenly said. "Quite petite. The impact when she bumped into me was more a dynamic of force rather than of weight."

"Well, that's a start. You should pass that on to Sibley. It might be a useful clue."

But Smy's face became fixed. "I will do no such thing. I have seen enough of Sibley to last me to the end of my days. I will find this woman myself."

Tranmer wryly smiled, knowing that this was just an excuse for Smy to investigate the murder on her own terms. He began to remonstrate with her that the matter was best left to the police but, realising that such a statement would have no impact at all on his friend, changed the subject. "You still haven't told me how you came to know Laurie Morrie. Was it when you first went to London? I do remember you once letting that slip."

"I knew someone else in the family first. It was through her that I met Morrie. Actually, his real name is Wright, Lawrence Wright."

"Oh, so Morrie's a stage name?"

"A stage name," confirmed Smy.

"And you became good friends, you and this Lawrence Wright?"

It was Smy's turn to stop walking this time. "Is this an official conversation? Am I talking to Herbert or Inspector Tranmer? I think I have a right to know."

Tranmer laughed. "Oh, it's definitely Herbert asking you. I'm just intrigued. The formidable and upright Miss Winifred Smy hobnobbing with a music hall star. I must be honest, I find it all quite difficult to imagine. Tell me, were you and this Wright..."

"No!" snapped Smy. "Don't you dare think anything of the sort for one moment."

"Apologies, apologies. It was just my little joke. So why do I detect so much animosity in your tone when you mention him?"

Smy walked briskly on. "Let us leave the subject there shall we?"

THE MYSTERIOUS MARGUERITE

A week had now passed since the fateful concert in Framlingham. Winifred Smy had not heard anything from the police and assumed that, whoever the suspects were, she was not one of them. But having been at the centre of the events that evening had left her plagued with worry. There was one fact that was absolutely clear in her mind: circumstances had been carefully arranged that night so as to incriminate her for the murder. After all, it was Morrie's manager, Alfred Carver, who had asked her to go to the dressing room. Why would he have done that? Yes, her relationship with Morrie had always been fractious, but she could not recall, all those years ago, having wronged Carver. Perhaps Carver's dedication, in his role as Morrie's manager, had changed him. Maybe he was acquiescent to whatever activity Morrie asked of him, however mendacious that activity might be.

Apparently, the local papers were still full of the story from that night, but Smy thought it best to avoid them. Manners, she thought, must have had a field day with the fact that the murderous event took place, not only on his doorstep, but when he had been present in the building. It then occurred to her that if there had been any developments in the murder case she, in her self-imposed isolation, would not be aware of them.

So where had Laurie Morrie - or Lawrence Wright for that matter - disappeared to? And what exactly did happen that night and why? Smy walked out into her back garden and mused over the progress of her vegetable beds. There were leeks and broccoli still to be harvested, but the chard had not been a success. So much for Spadger's enthusiastic endorsement of autumn sowing, she thought.

Her mind drifted back to a summer party in 1892 in a large north London villa on the Eyre estate. Who the house was owned by Smy couldn't remember, but she would never forget the look on Morrie's face when she arrived, his stony glare instantly communicating his anger at her appearance. He had turned to the woman he had been sitting and talking with, made his excuses and then came walking with great urgency across the lawn towards Smy. Smy, momentarily alarmed, had quickly gathered herself before asking, "Hello, Lawrence. I thought you'd…"

"Don't 'hello Lawrence' me, you…"

It was the cheery "helloooo" of the postman who snapped Miss Smy back into the present. Walking up Church Lane that ran alongside Miss Smy's back garden, he had suddenly spotted her and came stomping over, resting his postbag on Smy's garden wall.

"Post for me, Nathan?"

"Now let me see…I know there's a couple of…ah, there they are." Nathan Curdy extracted the two letters with a display of surprise at having located them so quickly. Curdy, a small, bald man whose facial features all seemed to have sunk to the lower half of his head, was notorious for having an utterly disorganised approach both to his work and his personal life.

A rumour still persisted in the local villages that his marriage to Mrs Curdy (as she now was) came as a complete surprise to him and that he still harboured doubts as to whether he had any knowledge of having actually met his wife before the day of his nuptials.

The other habit that Nathan Curdy had - and one which people found deeply irritating - was waiting with the post's recipient to see who the mail was from. Miss Smy, well used to this postal peccadillo, always responded with hearty thanks whilst quickly walking away.

Once she had seen that the disappointed postman had reluctantly carried on with his round, she looked at the postmarks of the letters to see from where they had been posted. She often wondered why she didn't just open the envelope and satisfy her curiosity quickly once and for all, but it was a habit she was reluctant to change.

The first envelope she knew to be from the milliners in Debenham; Hannah Bowman's beautiful handwriting con-firmed that. But the second envelope was a very different matter. It was buff-coloured and, Smy instantly noticed, of very good quality. She made her way back into the kitchen and reached for her letter opener. The letter itself had a slight grey tint and, as she unfolded it, she immediately found her eyes drawn to the embossed initials at the top: MDG. At the foot of the envelope was a small decoration of flowers.

My dearest Miss Smy

I would request the honour of your company at lunch in the Goring Hotel, Beeston Place, London S.W. on Thursday 6th May at 1.00 pm.

I am in possession of certain information that I am confident you

would wish to be made known to you.
   The favour of an answer is requested.
   Very sincerely
   Miss Marguerite De Gruchy

A look of intrigue was soon evident on Miss Smy's face and she carefully folded the letter and tapped it lightly against her chest whilst she considered it. It was not a name she recognised, but the fact that it had alluded to information she might 'wish to be made known' drew her to the conclusion that it must, in some way, be related to the murder at the Framlingham Assembly Hall.

Smy sat at her piano and played what she could remember of a Czerny exercise she had toiled with some years before. Her fingers delicately leapt across the keys although they did so with no thought from her, so ingrained into her being had those exercises from her adolescent years become.

Her mind kept returning to the same questions. Why did Morrie and Carver carefully arrange matters so as to implicate her? Was it revenge, perhaps? But why wait until now? Surely, if there was revenge to be sought, such opportunities in far less public circumstances would have been more successful. No, there was a reason why she had been selected and perhaps the writer of the letter she had just received might reveal just what the real reason was.

And then her mind settled on the unknown man who had been shot exactly where she had expected to find Morrie on the night she entered his dressing room. What was his involvement and why had matters been arranged so that he would be the victim and not Morrie? And how had Morrie managed to leave the Assembly Hall without being seen? And the biggest question of all, to which she constantly found herself returning, was: where was Morrie now?

Smy rose from the piano, opened a drawer in her dresser and took out her writing paper and envelopes.

THE NUNN'S STORY

"Can I help?"

Smy turned around and instantly recognised the face: it was one of the fiddlers who had made up the hastily assembled band for the charity concert. "Charlie?"

"It is, and I take it you're Miss Smy. Dew yew come in." Charlie Nunn led Miss Smy into the large auditorium of the Assembly Hall, a hall that was now strangely empty as their footsteps echoed around the walls. As Smy took in her surroundings, she found it hard to imagine that such traumatic events had so recently taken place within its high walls. Charlie came to a halt in the middle of the hall and rubbed his hands together to try and keep them warm. "Chilly, ain't it?"

Smy drew her jacket closer around her; the rays of a pale Spring sun had failed to penetrate into the hall and it was obvious that Charlie was hoping the conversation was not going to be a long one.

"You were playing at the concert, weren't you? Violin?"

"Fiddle. Violin. All the same, eh? In a pub, 'tis one, in a concert, 'tis another."

"And you look after the hall as well?"

Charlie looked around it once more, with a pride that suggested he might have built it entirely himself. "Keep it clean 'n' that. Teks some doin' I can tell yew."

"At the concert last week, Charlie, who was the man on the snare drum? Was that a friend?"

"Oh, him. The one that wuz killed? Never sin 'im afore. Didn't even come to the raherssals. Mind yew, if 'e 'ad, I'd a told 'im not t' bother comin' back. He weren't a mucher with that drum."

"So he just appeared on the night?"

"Aye. An' sat down as bold as brass like 'e wuz born to be there. 'E were 'bout two bars behind the song every time. Strewth, I told mesel', where in god's name did 'e shew up from?"

"When did you first notice him?"

Charlie rubbed the stubble on his chin and thought about Smy's question. "Furst notice 'im? Probably just as we were 'bout to get gooin'. I saw 'im and then caught the eye o' old Spurlin'..."

"Mr Spurling. The man who was conducting?"

"The same. Why 'e looked at me 'n' I looked at 'im and yew could tell we were thinken the same thing. 'Oo's this clown we got all a' sudden? I got to thinken 'e never played that snare drum in 'is life afore that night. Any chile you moight drag in off the street could dew better."

Smy was disappointed. She had meant to talk to Samuel Spurling at some point but now feared that if she did so, she would only elicit the same response.

"Mr Manners is supposed to be joining us as you know, but I can see he's already late. Could I ask you to show me the dressing room? The one where the murder took place."

"Well, Mr Manners assured me that I wuz to tek you both in t'gether. I don't loike the thought a just tekken only yew in there, Miss Smy. Now, no offence meant an' all."

"Oh, I'm quite grown up now," said Smy walking briskly over to where the rooms offstage were. An astonished Charlie Nunn soon went running after her. However, when Smy reached the door she found that it was still locked. She turned to Nunn and offered him her sweetest smile. "Shall you unlock or may I?"

Although both options seemed to contradict Charlie's assertion that they should wait for Manners' arrival, his befuddled mind gave way and he unlocked the door. Smy's first disappointment was to notice that the room had been emptied of its furniture. "Charlie, who set the dressing room up for Mr Morrie?"

"Thas me. Very particular 'e wuz. Very particular. But 'e is a star so, I s'ppose thas the way o' things."

"What sort of things did he ask for?"

"Oh, bottles o' water. Sanwidges. Ciggies."

"Woodbines?"

"Thas right. Wills Wild Woodbines, the list said. Very particular 'e wuz."

There was a rapid pattering of footsteps heard outside and then a collision followed by a sudden groan of someone in pain.

"Cood blaarst me. Whoever is that?"

Smy sighed and casually reassured Charlie Nunn, "Oh, don't worry, if I'm not mistaken that will be Mr Manners. I'm afraid he's permanently at war with his surroundings." Sure enough, a flustered Nigel Manners appeared in the doorway. With a twist of his scrawny neck, he attempted to compose himself.

"Most sorry. Got held up and couldn't get away. Oh, I hope I haven't broken the chair in the hall."

Charlie Nunn looked confused. "But it wuz the only chair in the hall!"

"Was it? Well, I was in such a hurry that I didn't see it until… well, until it was too late. Anyway, here now. Miss Smy, how are you?"

"I'm very good, thank you. These are more hospitable surroundings than when we were last together."

"Yes, indeed. Ah, I see they've cleared the room. That's disappointing. When you wrote to me to meet here, I had assumed that the room would be as it was on the night."

Smy walked slowly around the room. It was almost perfectly square, with the door into it almost at the junction where two sides of the square met. On the far side of the room was a sash window which, to Smy's eye, had not been opened for some time given the amount of cobwebs that were shrouding the window fastener.

"Charlie, other than the door, is this window the only way in or out of this room?"

"'Tis."

Smy started to walk the opposite way; there was no other exit that she could see. So how did Morrie leave the dressing room after the show? And how did they persuade the man who was now dead to become involved in the escapade that night?

"They've still not found him, Miss Smy. Or Carver. To use the vernacular, they've both 'done a bunk'. Disappeared without a trace. All very mysterious, I would say."

"And the man that was murdered, have the police found out who he was?"

Manners shook his head and sighed. "Not to my knowledge. He just seemed to show up on the night, played ineptly throughout the concert and then was found with a bullet in his back. I expect Charlie here has told you the same."

Smy walked purposefully to the centre of the room and stood quite still; only her head moved as she scanned the room. "Remind me, Charlie. The dressing table, such as it was, was against that wall. A mirror was propped up on the table and some lamps were arranged on either side so that Laurie Morrie could apply his make-up. Am I right?"

"Thas right, Miss Smy. And a wardrobe along the opp'site wall 'ere. And a coat stand in that corner." Nunn pointed to the corner which was diagonally opposite the door.

Smy looked carefully as he spoke, reimagining the room again and, with Charlie Nunn's direction, began to feel that a better picture of how everything was arranged on that fateful evening was slowly emerging.

"The wardrobe. That would have been directly behind the murdered man, would it not?"

"Roight enough, Miss Smy. It would."

"And where is the wardrobe now?"

"Back in Mr Spurling's house. 'E koindly lent it to the 'all for the night."

An appointment with Mr Spurling might be useful after all, thought Smy. She took in the room once more and then decided that she'd seen enough. As they were walking back through the hall, she lightheartedly told Manners about the luxuries that Morrie had insisted be in the room on the night.

"Thas right, Mr Manners. Sanwidges, ciggies, a few bottles of water. There were a couple of other things as well if I remember. Let me see…" Nunn reached inside his jacket and unfolded a letter to check his list.

"You kept the list?" asked Manners.

"Of course. I got Laurie Morrie hisself to autograph it. Here, see?"

"Charlie, would you mind if I took a closer look at that list of yours?"

"This list? Why o' course, Miss Smy. 'Ere you go."

The specific requirements for the night were exactly as Charlie had remembered; the other two items that he had failed to recall were a toothbrush and a small towel. But it wasn't the list of items that most caught the eye of Miss Smy. It was the distinctive monogram embossed at the top of the page bearing the letters 'MDG'.

REACH HITHER THY FINGER

"Hannah, I believe we've all finished. Could you take the plates away?"

The Reverend Pilbeam's servant collected the empty dinner plates with the confident aplomb of a silver service waitress. Pilbeam rose and offered to top up Miss Smy's wine, which she politely refused. He then turned to Agatha, his wife, who said, "Just a little more, please."

"It's good to finish it. An excellent claret. Only one left in the cellar I'm afraid and what with the war and everything, we're unlikely to bag ourselves another case for a while." Pilbeam looked up to make sure that Hannah had left the room before returning to his seat. "My dear Miss Smy, you have been through quite an ordeal."

"It wasn't the evening I was planning to have."

"But how do you know this Laurie Morrie? I was up in town just before Christmas and he was quite the thing. Posters all over the place."

"It was his sister, Eleanor, I knew first, Agatha. We met at a concert. And then it was through Eleanor that I met Lawrence."

"Lawrence? Doesn't everyone call him Laurie?"

"His real name is Lawrence Wright and, as you saw for yourself, he has become rather famous. However, Eleanor

Wright is the person I first met and was a very talented violinist. I have to say, though, that they moved in quite different circles when I came to know them both. At that time, Lawrence was bottom-of-the-bill variety and Eleanor's star was very much in the ascendant in the world of classical music."

"Are you still in contact with her?"

"No. We…we all went our separate ways. Anyway, that's all a long time ago now. This is a very good claret, Mr Pilbeam; I feel quite honoured that you should share it with me."

Pilbeam would have none of it and waved the compliment away. "Not at all. We were just so relieved to hear that the charges had been dropped and that you had been safely returned to the bosom of Kenton. Now tell me, because both Agatha and I know you of old, what do you think really happened at that concert? From what I understand, and I must add the caveat that the purveyor of the gossip was a most unreliable rector, a man was murdered by a bullet meant for our famous music hall star. And the gun was then planted on a poor Miss Smy who had happened to enter the room just after the shot was fired. How close is that to the truth?"

Smy finished the last of her wine before patting her lips with her napkin. "All true. Your rector is not as unreliable as you suppose."

"And this Laurie Morrie," interposed Mrs Pilbeam, "has fled the scene and can't be found?"

"Nor his manager, a Mr Alfred Carver. Someone else I've also known for many years."

Pilbeam leaned conspiratorially forward, saying with a lowered voice, "But this all sounds like a carefully arranged plot to incriminate you for murder. Whatever have you done that would drive these fellows to such a thing?"

Smy suddenly felt uncomfortable. "Oh, I'm sure that my misfortune was to enter the room at a very inopportune moment. It could just as likely have been someone else who had entered the room at the time the man was shot."

To Miss Smy's relief, Pilbeam - satisfied with her answer - nodded his agreement before leaving the room to ask Hannah to serve the dessert. Whilst Smy and Agatha Pilbeam were waiting, the latter attended to a sputtering candle on the sideboard. "That must have been a terrible time for you. I can't imagine how you coped being accused of such a thing."

"I won't lie to you, Agatha, there were some moments where I did rather fear the worst. Thankfully, the case against me didn't stand up to any real scrutiny, but it was all very alarming to say the least. I went to the Assembly Hall only today…"

Pilbeam bustled back into the room. "Won't be long. Two minutes or so and we will all be enjoying our just desserts!"

"Miss Smy was saying that she revisited the scene of the crime today."

"Really? At the Assembly Hall? That was rather brave of you. Any particular reason?"

"Curiosity. No more than that."

The good reverend looked unconvinced. "Reach hither thy finger, and behold my hands; and reach hither thy hand, and thrust it into my side: and be not faithless, but believing."

"You think me a doubting Thomas?"

"I do. From what I understand, the man who was shot wasn't known to anyone, including your good self. The dreadful thing you went through is over and you have been exonerated, but one now learns that you still chose to return to the scene of the crime. Why? Because you, like our good man, Didymus, cannot live until he satisfies his doubt."

"Putting that allusion aside, it was a useful visit. And, whether I like it or not, I am involved in one way or another. So, yes, perhaps I am your doubting Thomas and there is much I need to understand about everything that happened that night."

"So what do you plan to do next?" asked Agatha Pilbeam.

"I thought it might be worthwhile paying Mr Spurling a visit."

Pilbeam audibly groaned as he sat down. "Oh, not the great Framlingham musical maestro, Samuel Spurling?"

Smy seemed surprised. "You know him?"

"Yes, unfortunately, I do. Two years ago, I helped out at St Michael's when Sampson, the vicar there, was ill. Samuel Spurling ran the church choir and was irredeemably pompous. Kept wittering on endlessly about being short of money. I found it very difficult holding my tongue at times. How Sampson puts up with him, I'll never know. Besides, how can Spurling help? From what I understand, he just happened to be conducting a very indifferent orchestra on the night when all these terrible things happened."

"Well, I have questions that perhaps he might help me with. For example, why did he allow someone who obviously had no musical talent to just turn up and join his orchestra? Yes, they were a hotchpotch of musicians that night, but most could play to a decent standard. And why should he have lent his wardrobe to the hall for the two evenings Laurie Morrie was booked to perform? That struck me as rather odd."

Hannah re-entered the room, put her large tray down on the table and placed a plate before each of the three diners.

"Ah, treacle pudding! And do you know that Hannah here uses the very same recipe my mother used? I always implore

Hannah not to stint on the time it must be steamed: three hours at least I tell her."

His wife rolled her eyes and smiled patiently. "It's the same story every time, Winifred. Personally, I think Hannah's treacle pudding is far superior to the ones my husband's mother used to make, god rest her soul."

"That can't be true. It's the same ingredients, the same instructions. How can one be superior to the other? What do you think, Miss Smy?"

"I have always thought that the food of our youth tastes better when it has a little nostalgia sprinkled over it, Reverend."

"Hmph! I refuse to give way on this. Anyway, to return to all these unfortunate events, do tell me how your meeting with Spurling goes. I never enjoyed a single conversation I ever had with that man. A very prickly so-and-so, believe me."

"Apparently he lives in a very nice house on Double Street. Do you happen to know what he does for a living?"

Pilbeam looked up from the bottle of dessert wine he had just uncorked. "If I remember right, he claimed to be a music examiner, which I found a little strange as the only thing I ever saw him involved in was the choir at St. Michael's. So he seems to be receiving some income from somewhere, but I have no idea what that source is."

"I'm looking forward all the more to meeting him. Our Framlingham conductor sounds like quite an intriguing man. Oh, before I forget, can I borrow your *Debrett's*?"

"The Peerage? Of course, but you must tell me why you want it. Perhaps you are about to discover you are descended from some obscure but privileged heritage?"

"If I do discover that it has been only blue blood coursing through my veins all these years, then you and Agatha shall be the first to know. No, it's just a little preparation I need to do for yet another appointment, and a rather elevated one at that. I'm meeting someone at the Goring Hotel."

"The Goring in Belgravia? Well, my treacle pudding will not be able to compete with the fine dining you'll be offered there. What say you, my dearest?"

"Who is your appointment with? I would love to know."

"Well, Agatha, let's just say that I already suspect she might not be quite all she appears to be."

MEETING MISS DE GRUCHY

Winifred Smy was beginning to feel that the supercilious waiter who had shown her to her table suspected that she had been stood up. Although his manners were perfect and the curve of his spine elegantly perpendicular, there was a slight - almost imperceptible - raising of his eyebrows communicating an opinion that Smy's presence was an awkward one. A rather ornate grandfather clock at the far end of the dining room told Smy that Miss Marguerite de Gruchy was already twenty minutes late. She looked out of the window at a view which reminded her that, for all its overweening sense of self-worth, London could often be a grey and charmless city.

"I am just so terribly, terribly sorry." Smy was caught off-guard and the rapid shuffling of expensive cloth being trailed across the hotel's restaurant carpet announced the arrival of her luncheon guest. "Please, don't get up. It is so rude of me to be so late. Terribly rude. You must think me awfully impolite. Have you a drink? Let us have an aperitif. Two vodkas please. Do you drink vodka? Oh, you must do. It is quite the thing. Three or four years ago we watched the *Ballets Russe* and I had my first vodka. It was dear Diaghilev himself who poured me my first glass. Such a darling! What a man. Quite unbelievable. And those dancers!"

Miss Smy remained still and carefully eyed her luncheon partner. She was, undoubtedly, a striking woman. The first thing that no one could fail to notice was the size of the hat that she had wearily taken off and held suspended in mid-air until one of the waiting staff took it from her. Miss de Gruchy's loose white blouse was so different to the figure-hugging blouses that Smy remembered when she first observed the latest fashions in London. Although small in stature, Smy couldn't help but be impressed by the self-confidence that she irradiated to all around her.

"I'm very glad to meet you, Miss de Gruchy. I was beginning to fear I had the wrong instructions for today."

But Marguerite de Gruchy's mind was still distracted by the need to order the two vodkas, and soon the disapproving waiter was taking her order. "Sorry, what was that you said, Miss Smy?"

Smy continued to smile in the right places as Miss de Gruchy conversed. She was, Smy thought, probably in her late twenties. Her eyes vividly green, her nose irritatingly perfect. There was something sullen about the mouth, especially the way that the very corners of her lips pointed downwards. But she was, as Spadger had often put it, 'a damnably 'andsome mawther'.

They spoke whilst waiting for the lunch to arrive, neither woman venturing beyond topics of conversation that might prove awkward: the progress of the war, the indifferent weather and the apparent installation of central heating in all of the Goring Hotel's rooms.

Once lunch had arrived, Miss de Gruchy took her napkin and folded it in half, carefully ensuring that the crease of the napkin nestled against her blouse. Smy, after maintaining the air of forced politeness for some time, decided to come to the point. "In your invitation, you said that you had certain information that you would wish to be made known to me. I confess to being somewhat intrigued by what this information might be."

This time it was Marguerite de Gruchy who scrutinised her luncheon partner. Putting down her knife and fork she glanced briefly at the neighbouring tables before asking, "What I am about to say must remain a secret. Will you give me your promise that you will not pass on to anyone what I wish to tell you?"

"Then you must not tell me. I am not minded to give assurances about information I do not know."

Miss de Gruchy wiped her hands delicately on her napkin. "If I were to inform you that Lawrence Wright and I are to be married then you would think nothing of it. But my father would think a great deal of it. A woman of my social status marrying a man who is not only my social inferior…"

"But a theatre performer as well?" suggested Smy.

"It's quite a predicament I find myself in, wouldn't you agree?"

"Am I to understand that you have invited me to lunch just to inform me that you and Mr Wright are to be married? Why ever would you invite me, of all people, to be told that?"

"No, but I wanted you to know that my interest in his welfare is rooted in the most tender feelings."

Smy was careful not to allow her face to reflect the confusion that she was feeling as Miss de Gruchy spoke, continuing to slowly sip water from her glass to help her retain her composure. "First, I must congratulate you on your engagement, although you must be suffering a great deal of anxiety given the events of the other evening in Framlingham. Tell me, where is

Lawrence now?"

De Gruchy looked down towards her lap where her trembling hands worried away at her napkin. "I wish I knew. You see, that's why I wanted to see you. I heard that you were accused of trying to kill Lawrence but the man posing as the drummer was killed in his stead. That poor man. And Alfred Carver is missing too. Tell me, do you think they are alive?"

"I can't say. You see, Miss de Gruchy, I only know as much as you. Does Lawrence have any enemies?"

"Oh, good god, yes. Lots of enemies. He's a very determined man and I am certain that there have been people that he has upset along the way. But has he upset someone to the extent that they would want to kill him? That seems a step too far."

Smy began to experience the uncomfortable feeling that her table was being watched. Whilst a tearful Miss de Gruchy was looking out of the window, Smy, pretending to look for the waiter, took the opportunity to discreetly view the neighbouring tables, all of which were now taken. Outwardly, every person seemed preoccupied with their own meals, but the niggling doubt persisted all the same. It was the voice of her luncheon partner that drew her back into the conversation.

"So, other than what I have read in the papers, is there nothing you could add that might lighten this awful state I find myself in, not knowing whether Lawrence is alive or where he might be?"

"I'm surprised that you think I would know more than you. Before the concert in Framlingham, I had not seen Lawrence for many years and when we did know each other the relationship we had was, shall we say, rather strained."

De Gruchy looked up with, what seemed to Smy, genuine surprise. "Oh, he didn't tell me that. He told me you were very good friends with his sister, Eleanor. What did you fall out about?"

At that moment the waitress appeared with the lunch and carefully laid their next course before them. It seemed that once Miss de Gruchy had ascertained that Smy knew no more than she, her demeanour reverted to the breezy behaviour she had shown when she first arrived. As they rose to leave the table, Smy asked, "If I do find out any more information, it would be good to have an address where I may write to you."

"That would be an enormous help to me. As you may have gathered, the police have been in contact with me on several occasions convinced that I know where Lawrence might be. I am also convinced that they are reading my correspondence. May I ask you a great favour? Should you chance upon any information that you think might give me some hope, would you send it to a very good friend of mine? Her name is Miss Armscott. Polly Armscott. She's a secretary at Admiralty House and utterly trustworthy and discreet. Shall I write down the address?"

"There's no need. Admiralty House? It's Whitehall, if I remember right?"

"You know it?"

"I knew it many years ago."

Smy and Miss de Gruchy parted outside the hotel entrance where two gentlemen were also taking their leave of each other, making loud promises to meet up once again. Smy didn't fail to notice that as she and Miss de Gruchy went their separate ways, the two male friends likewise separated with each following their respective quarry at a careful distance.

SPURNED BY SPURLING

Samuel Spurling's house on Double Street sat snugly amongst a long line of residences that almost seemed like a museum's display of housing styles through the centuries. With a cream brick frontage, it had a pleasing symmetry with two sash windows on each level and a pedimented door that sat haughtily above several steps. The curtains downstairs were drawn but Smy decided still to see if Spurling was at home and knocked the door with two firm raps. Eventually, the door was yanked open and a tall, thick-set man barked, "What is it!"

"Mr Spurling?"

The man looked suspiciously at Smy before returning with, "Who are you?"

"My name is Winifred Smy. I was given to understand that you might be able to help me."

There was no doubt that Spurling knew her name and his pale blue eyes surveyed her with an icy disdain. He bore the face of a man whose features had been puffed out by too much good living, with a ruddiness that had spread from his cheeks to now encompass the unmistakable blotched nose of a regular drinker. "Is this about the murder at the Assembly Hall? If so, I will not detain you a moment longer."

Smy held her hand up against the door. "Oh no, Mr Spurling.

I am looking for a teacher in music harmony and was given your name by Reverend Pilbeam. He was adamant that there wasn't a finer teacher to be had. You may remember that he once deputised for Mr Sampson when he took ill."

With this information, Spurling became less guarded. "Pilbeam? Yes, I think I do remember Pilbeam. Look, now is not a good time I…err…I am giving a lesson at the moment. Could you call back in an hour? We can talk then. But I warn you, my fees will be higher than those charged by other tutors."

Having agreed to call back at just after eleven o'clock, Smy walked back towards Framlingham's Market Square, bent on purchasing a newspaper and a pot of tea. However, once she came out into Church Street, a small voice within her seemed to be urging her to return to the Assembly Hall and, with it being so close to where she stood, she turned her steps towards it once more.

She could hear Charlie Nunn whistling just inside the entrance and, catching his eye, signalled that she would like to come inside.

"Carn't keep away, eh?"

"Something like that, Charlie. I know this is probably asking too much, but I would like to look in that dressing room just once more. I won't be more than a couple of minutes, I promise."

Charlie Nunn rubbed the top of his head without removing his cap, his hand sliding back and forth beneath it like a magician teasing an audience. "Well, I guess it's alright. But it'll still be the same as last toime, y' know. Oh, hello sir." Charlie was now looking over Smy's shoulder and she turned to see that he was talking to Herbert Tranmer, who was just passing. It was then Smy noticed that he was with a woman who had her hand on his arm.

"Miss Smy! What are you doing here, as if I need to ask?"

Smy smiled and glanced at Tranmer's female companion. "You must be Maud. Herbert has told me all about you. I'm Winifred, Winifred Smy." Despite her best efforts, Smy felt that there was something restrained about her emotions as she greeted Maud. The warmth that she tried to convey felt forced and heavy-handed. She also became aware that there was a similar awkwardness in Maud's manner.

"It's good to meet you, Miss Smy. Herbert has told me so many interesting things about you." The delivery of the comment was undeniably flat and without feeling. Tranmer, as if sensing the atmosphere that had pervaded the exchange, interrupted with, "Well, I was just walking Maud to her mother's. She lives just off the square. We won't keep you. Good day, Miss Smy."

Smy watched as Tranmer and his new partner walked away and became conscious that she was wrestling with a feeling she didn't quite understand. Was it jealousy? Perhaps it was the realisation that she was now witnessing the aftermath of a decision that had been hers alone. She shook her head as if to make the uncomfortable thoughts disappear and turned back to Charlie. "I'm sorry. Can I look at the room again?"

Charlie Nunn led her back to the room and watched whilst she looked around once more at the empty space. No, she decided, there was nothing new to be seen. She was hoping that a second visit might allow her a fresh insight, perhaps noticing something that had eluded her the first time. But all was as it had been before. She looked back to Charlie and indicated that her survey had been a fruitless one.

"I'm seeing Mr Spurling this morning. I'm sure it will

prove a pointless errand but it will at least satisfy my need for completeness in everything. You said that he had lent his own wardrobe on the night the man was shot. When did you return it? Do you remember?"

"Oh yes. Clear as day, I remember. Monday morning after the weekend. First thing. Y'see, we 'ad to git it out of the way."

"Out of the way? What for?"

"For the lads tha' were comin' to do the decoratin'."

Smy turned towards Charlie and narrowed her eyes. "Decorating? I didn't know that the room had been decorated."

"Only the back wall, Miss Smy."

Smy slowed her step and carefully took in what she was hearing. At the far end of the hall a door opened and Herbert Tranmer entered. "Well, what did you think?"

Smy, who was still turning over the very recent revelation of Charlie Nunn, was caught unawares by the question. "Think about what, Herbert?"

"Not what but whom, Winifred. What did you think about Miss Clemence?"

Smy rallied her thoughts and answered with an enthusiastic, "Oh, very lovely. Very lovely, indeed." Again, she felt that the words were hollow as she spoke them. Thankfully, Herbert Tranmer seemed satisfied with what she had said. There was an air of boyishness about his pleasure that threw Smy, and she found herself conflicted in a way that she had never felt before. Tranmer's manner had an attractiveness that, up to now, she had failed to notice, and she caught herself looking at him as if for the first time.

"I hope you don't mind me asking, Winifred. Your opinion of Miss Clemence means a lot to me."

Smy was anxious to change the subject; Tranmer's soliciting

of her acceptance of Maud felt distinctly uncomfortable. "I'm going to see Mr Spurling, Herbert. He was the conductor of the small orchestra on the night of the shooting."

"Spurling? Oh, I know him. He's a bit..." Tranmer raised an eyebrow as if such a gesture would discreetly impart his opinion where words might fail.

"I'm not due to meet him for another half hour. Are you free at all? I would welcome a chance to share one or two things."

Within minutes, Smy and Tranmer were walking slowly along the road that led out of Framlingham towards Saxmundham. The clouds had lifted themselves high and were now scrapes of grey-white against the ice-blue sky. Smy related her encounter with Miss de Gruchy the previous day.

"Well, you do seem to find yourself in very elevated circles, Winifred. De Gruchy sounds like a very grand name."

"There's nothing grand about our Miss de Gruchy, Herbert. It was all a sham, from start to finish."

"Sham? What do you mean, a sham?"

"A sham. She is no more a woman of the exalted peerage as is Edith Gladwell. The letter was the first clue. I have it here...give me a moment...there you are." Smy handed the letter to Tranmer, who stopped walking and scrutinised it carefully.

"Looks fine to me."

"Oh no. There were two errors that I instantly noticed. You'll remember that I once told you about my time as a Governess working for Lord Kenilworth's family. One soon learns a great deal about the etiquette of the privileged classes."

"Right. Well, as someone who is severely lacking the etiquette of the privileged classes, what is supposed to be wrong with this letter?"

Smy took the letter from Tranmer and pointed to the word 'lunch'. "One would never refer to it as 'lunch'; a midday meal is always 'luncheon'."

Tranmer looked doubtful. "Luncheon? Are you sure?"

"Oh, quite sure."

Tranmer took back the letter and read through it once more. "You said there were two things. What was the second?"

"The name. The de Gruchy family always spells the 'de' with a lowercase 'd'. As you can see, it is quite clearly capitalised in both her signature and the embossed capitals at the top of the paper.

"But you still met this woman? This Miss de Gruchy?"

"Most certainly. My curiosity was piqued. And these blunders in her correspondence were amplified when I met her."

Tranmer handed the letter back to Smy and continued walking. "Enlighten me. What was it about her that gave her away?"

"The napkin."

Tranmer looked back at Smy with an incredulous stare. "Her napkin? Are you serious?"

"Quite serious. You don't seem to realise that there exists an eclectic set of codes by which the upper classes can distinguish the genuine members of the aristocracy from the aspiring upper middle classes. For those who view themselves as superior to all others, these codes are elaborate rings of defence that betray the interloper. Our Miss de Gruchy was an obvious interloper."

"Be that as it may, what's a napkin going to give away about someone?"

Smy took out a clean handkerchief and sat on the low brick

garden wall of a cottage. "Watch closely. You see, when a man sits down to a meal, he will fold his napkin in half with the crease towards him. But when a woman sits down to a meal and arranges a napkin on her lap, she folds it like this with the crease always away from her. Then, when she feels the need to dab the corners of her mouth, the crumbs from her meal will discreetly fall inside the napkin."

"So, if she's not who she says she is, then who is she?"

Smy rose from the garden wall and folded the handkerchief back into her bag. "I think I know and will ask Mr Manners to verify my suspicions with his insuperable network of colleagues. By the way, have you identified the murdered man yet?"

Tranmer looked away, seemingly embarrassed by Smy's question. "From what Sibley had told me, no, we still don't know who it was." Taking his watch from his waistcoat pocket, Tranmer advised, "I think we best be heading back to the town. You told me you have an appointment to keep."

Smy and Tranmer walked quickly back to Framlingham. Tranmer suggested that he would accompany Smy to Spurling's house as Double Street wasn't out of his way at all. Reaching the house, they were surprised to find the front door slightly ajar but Smy knocked just the same. With no audible response from inside the house, she knocked again. Once more, no sound was heard from within. She gently pushed the door back and leaned in, lustily shouting a cheery 'hello' to see if there might be a response.

Looking down the hallway, they noticed an outstretched arm on the floor protruding from one of the rooms just off the hallway. Both she and Tranmer rushed in and found Spurling in a pool of blood that was slowly solidifying in the room's carpet. Spurling's neck was a collar of bloody stab wounds and appeared to be the only source for all of the bloodstains. Tranmer immediately pulled back the cuff of Spurling's shirt sleeve and felt for a pulse. "My god, whoever attacked him must have been frenzied. Just look at his neck. I wonder how long he's been dead."

"Well, I would say not long at all. I left him only an hour ago. He told me he was with a pupil and suggested I should call back. I suspect that his pupil may have been a convenient fiction, Inspector."

"Inspector? I thought we were on first name terms."

"We were, but now you find yourself thrust back into your work and appear to have a second murder on your hands."

THE SLAUGHTERER'S HANDIWORK

Tranmer asked Winifred Smy if she would stay with Spurling's body to make sure that the crime scene was not compromised, whilst he ran to the nearby police station on Market Hill to ask for assistance. After twenty minutes or so, as she came down the stairs from a brief inspection of Spurling's bedrooms, she heard the creak of the front door being gently opened. But it wasn't Tranmer she found furtively peering in but Nigel Manners, in a high state of excitement.

"Ah, Miss Smy! I was just outside and heard someone moving around in the house. I naturally thought it was a policeman guarding the body. Is it true? Has Spurling really been murdered? Someone who was waiting in the police station has just burst into our office with the news." Manners looked past Smy and saw Spurling's lifeless outstretched arm. "Ooh, may I have a closer look?"

"No, you may not, Manners."

It wasn't Smy who refused the request but Tranmer who had just returned with a constable. After assigning the constable to guard the body until the doctor arrived, Tranmer motioned to Manners and Smy that he was going to accompany them both away from the crime scene. Already, on the opposite side of

Double Street, a huddle of neighbours had started to linger in small groups, eagerly eyeing Spurling's house. And as with all local gossiping, opinions and theories were being exchanged as to what had just happened.

Smy, Tranmer, and Manners walked slowly back to the Market square, with Manners feverishly jotting down all that Tranmer was able to tell him which, on the face of it, didn't amount to very much.

"Do you think that the murder is linked to the man who was shot in the Assembly Hall?"

"There is nothing to suggest that either death is linked, Mr Manners, or even that the demise of Mr Spurling is a murder. You used that word, not me. We will want to consider all possibilities and would request that caution be applied until we have studied the doctor's report and thoroughly investigated the crime scene."

"You mean it might be suicide instead? Or an accident?"

"I mean that everyone would be advised to exercise restraint until we have all of the facts before us."

Manners grew agitated and shook his pad and pencil in a fit of pique. "Come on, Inspector, you can do better than that. I can't go back with the biggest story of the day and write five hundred words about waiting for a doctor's report. My editor will have my guts for garters if I use those constabulary phrases. Give me something I can hook my readers with."

"Mr Manners, you are able enough to raise the county's temperature about Spurling's death; I can only give you my official view. You are already ahead of the other papers with this, so I'm sure that that in itself will warm your editor's ice-cold heart."

Once Manners had loped away brimming with the excitement of his exclusive, Tranmer asked if Smy would care for a walk around the castle. But Smy demurred, pointing out that it might appear unseemly for someone like him who was so well known to be seen with anyone other than his new partner.

"But that's ridiculous. I only want to ask for your thoughts about Spurling. It's a purely professional conversation."

"Maybe so, but the appearance of our intercourse, as innocent as we both know it will be, might encourage a very different conclusion from people, and you and Miss Clemence do not deserve that."

"Well, I suppose you're right. Anyway, this is Sibley's case so I suppose I shouldn't be meddling. But let me just ask you one question. You said that when you first called on Spurling, he told you that he was with somebody. Did he say who?"

"No, just that he was giving a lesson and it was not a good time."

"And you didn't see who he was teaching?"

"The downstairs curtains were closed, which might mean everything and nothing. If you should see him, then it would be helpful to point Inspector Sibley towards Spurling's appointments book. It was on the sideboard and, with so much time to kill whilst I waited for you to return, I couldn't resist the temptation to view what appointments he had for the day."

"And what you noticed was that, curiously, there was no appointment in his book for this morning. Is that a fair conclusion?"

Smy smiled enigmatically and chose not to answer, instead looking up at the sky, noticing that the wind had increased and a band of dark clouds was slowly bulging above the roofs of the square. "I think rain might be a possibility, Herbert."

"And what else caught your eye whilst left alone in Spurling's house?"

"Oh, Herbert, you seem to think me overly inquisitive. I might be offended if I didn't know you so well. You're the Inspector and who am I? Why, just a lowly citizen who is always happy to support her gallant local constabulary."

"Except for the fact that, when you do notice something, you forget to inform your gallant local constabulary."

"Unless my memory has become suddenly faulty, there have been several instances where my information was ignored by that same gallant local constabulary. Perhaps you would like me to list them for you?"

Tranmer held up his hands in acknowledgement of Smy's point. "Very true, very true. But tell me, what else did you notice and I will make sure that it goes straight back to our dear Mr Sibley."

"A couple of things but, and I'm not being fey here, I need to think it all through first. One thing that certainly caught my eye was the technique employed by Spurling's attacker. I can't say anything more than I seemed to recognise the slaughterer's handiwork."

There was an audible sigh from Tranmer as he resigned himself to the fact that Smy was gently putting up a high wall around her thinking. "OK. I'll leave all that with you. Anyway, as this is Sibley's show I will leave it to him to get what he can from you. Where are you off to now?"

"The Assembly Hall. I need to satisfy my curiosity about something."

"How do you know it will be open?"

"Oh, that's not a worry. What I need to establish won't necessitate me having to trouble Charlie Nunn. Oh, before you go, can I make a request?"

"Of course. What is it?"

"Would you be available this time next week to play a duet in the Hall?"

Tranmer's eyes widened with surprise. "I'm sorry, Winifred. Do you want me to play in a concert or something?"

"Oh, no," Smy laughed. "Nothing like that. Just to go through a couple of old things we've already done. A little Mozart, perhaps? Only you and I. Although you can bring Miss Clemence along as well, if you like."

Tranmer's face clouded and he looked away. "I'm not sure that's a good idea. Maud told me she doesn't find music very interesting."

"Doesn't like music? Miss Clemence? That won't do, Herbert. Oh no, that won't do at all."

IN PURSUIT

As Smy had managed to catch the earlier train to London, she decided that the hour's walk to Whitehall would do her good. The rail journey had been wearing, particularly so as one man had smoked a large cigar that filled the small space with its odious smell. Yes, she concluded, the chance to clear her lungs and think would be an excellent idea.

She decided to walk the greater part of the route along the Embankment, stopping several times to view the myriad barges that crept along the river, carrying food and wares for London's man and beast. Along the stretch of the banked wall beneath her were several boats which had been tethered or anchored, lazily lifting and falling with the swell of the water.

Two days before, Smy had written:

My dearest Miss Armscott

I am coming up to town to visit some friends and was wondering if you might be able to meet with me for a short walk. There is some information I wish you to relate to Miss Marguerite de Gruchy and is such that I cannot trust it to paper.

I was hoping that you might be free at 12.30 pm on Thursday 13th May but fear that you may not be able to leave your place of work at this time. If you are available, then I will be waiting outside the Whitehall entrance to the Admiralty Building.

I would be most grateful if you could let me know whether this would be convenient or not.

Yours very sincerely
Miss Winifred Smy

Smy had received a reply the very next day from Miss Armscott to say that she would be happy to meet, but would not be willing to meet on the same terms again. Smy dutifully took up her position outside the entrance and, looking down at the clock of Big Ben, could see that she was still six minutes early. An instinct rose immediately within her as she waited and, remaining calm, Smy took out a small compact and pretended to smooth her eyebrow. The mirror revealed what she suspected, that a man was standing across the street scanning a newspaper. Smy knew him to be the same man who had followed Marguerite de Gruchy when they had both left The Goring Hotel.

"Miss Smy?"

Smy looked up to see a tall, thin woman with large blue eyes looking at her.

"Miss Armscott?"

"Indeed. It's good to meet you. It's a fine day for a walk. Shall we head towards Trafalgar Square?"

Smy felt a small glow of satisfaction. She had been quite confident that Marguerite de Gruchy and Miss Armscott were one and the same person, and that the suggestion of communicating through Armscott was a device to fool her into thinking that they were separate people. She was certain that this woman was not Polly Armscott.

"I understand that you have a message for me to pass on to

Miss de Gruchy."

"Do you know Miss de Gruchy?"

"I'm afraid I can't answer any of your questions. I am happy to take your message and then must get back to the office. As you will know, we are having a rather busy time of it just now."

Smy looked around to see if the man she had spotted on the other side of Whitehall had followed them but he was still standing at the same place where she had first seen him.

"I won't ask any more questions. My message is simply this: Lawrence Wright is to be married."

Miss Armscott looked around with raised eyebrows, but limited her answer to, "I will let her know." Armscott abruptly left Smy and walked briskly away. Smy walked on, and finding a newspaper carousel on the pavement, spun it slowly around to afford her a better view of the waiting man. He had remained where he was and seemed to be showing no interest in Smy at all, still studying his paper with keen interest.

She thought carefully about the situation and decided to buy a paper herself, and noticing a small café by the newsagents, managed to obtain a table where she had a good view of the waiting man. But what ensued was a long, long wait for them both and they were each presented with the same problem, how to eke out the long hours in their respective positions without raising any suspicion.

For the man in the street, this wasn't too difficult. He could saunter along the pavement for quite some distance whilst always having the entrance to the Admiralty Building within sight. But for Smy, she was compelled to lie to the owner of the café - a kind-faced, stout man with a stubble that was flecked with grey, peppery specks - that she was waiting for a close friend and had arrived far too early. She made two pots of tea and a tasteless bun stretch themselves over the long three and a half hours, whilst reading every column inch of her newspaper.

Just as the clock behind the serving counter had crept past five o'clock, she looked up to see that the man had gone. She leapt up and hurried towards the Admiralty entrance, rushing past the many people who had now finished work for the day and were making for the trams and tube. She kept looking upwards and, to her relief, spotted the man's dark brown coat. Alternating between rapid walking and short bursts of running, she managed to catch up so that she was always between ten and fifteen yards behind.

The man's newspaper now protruded from his coat pocket, and Smy looked carefully to see who he might be following. Looking beyond the man, she could make out several women and it was difficult to ascertain whom his attention was focused on. As they walked further down Whitehall the number of people ahead remained constant with various individuals joining or departing, which allowed Smy to winnow down the number of possible suspects. Soon, Smy had worked out that there were only two possible targets ahead, both walking quickly towards Parliament Square.

Conscious that the man might become aware that he, the hunter, was also being hunted, Smy began to create a more discreet distance between herself and the man. Suddenly, one of the women waved her hand to someone walking towards her and was soon met by a man who was obviously well known to her. The man Smy was following ignored the woman and walked on, and it was then that Smy could see just who he was pursuing: a well-dressed woman of petite stature, energetically walking towards Westminster tube station.

At the station entrance Smy was faced with two problems, maintaining a distance from the man so that he remained unaware of her following him, as well as making sure that the woman didn't become aware of her as well. As the three walked in turn onto the platform, Smy took the opportunity to interpose herself between the two, keeping slightly behind the line of both so as to remain undetected. The woman looked along the platform upon hearing the unmistakable rattle and rush of air that told everyone that the next train was about to arrive. And it was then that Smy finally satisfied her earlier suspicion: it was the very same woman who had pretended to be Miss Marguerite de Gruchy. As Smy had guessed, it was not the real Miss Armscott who had kept the lunchtime appointment, because the man had taken no notice of her when she had met Miss Smy. And the fact that he had remained at his post all afternoon proved that the real Miss Armscott was still in the building and yet to emerge.

The trio's underground train took them westward, first to Earl's Court tube station, where they changed to the District Line, alighting two stations later at Walham Green station. Thankfully for Smy, the pavements were still busy and she could follow both parties as they walked into Dawes Road. Miss Armscott reached for a key and let herself into a large house that bore all the hallmarks of having been converted into a number of small flats.

Once she had disappeared inside, the man looked at his fob watch before taking some detailed notes in a small pocket book. Seemingly satisfied that he had run his quarry to ground, he turned and walked towards - and then past - Miss Smy, giving no indication that he knew he'd been followed by her.

Once he'd turned the corner back to the Underground

station, Smy walked up to the house that she had seen Miss Armscott disappear into. Inside the open porch lay some mail which Smy quickly went through. There didn't seem to be any addressed to a Miss Armscott or, come to that, to Miss de Gruchy. She rapped the door knocker and took one step back. Through the pane of frosted glass she could see an arc of light spill out onto the hallway floor. The door was cautiously opened a small way, with an elderly woman's face peering suspiciously around it. Smy asked cheerily, "Does Miss Armscott live here? I have something for her which she left at the office."

The woman studied Smy's face carefully before she replied. "Miss Armscott? There's no one livin' 'ere of that name, dearie."

"A small woman. Late twenties. I've just watched Miss Armscott enter your house."

"You must be seein' fings, my love. It's only men what's taken my rooms, 'n' I won't 'ave no women canoodlin' and whatnot wiv 'em."

Smy swallowed hard and decided that either the woman was lying or she genuinely didn't realise that Miss Armscott had entered her house only minutes before. It felt bitterly disappointing to have unravelled one mystery - that Miss Armscott and Miss de Gruchy were the same person - only to be instantly met by another. She wished the woman well and walked back towards the station. As she walked beneath the entrance arcade into the booking hall, she heard a voice behind her ask, "Miss Winifred Smy?"

Smy turned around to see that she was now standing face to face with the very man she had just been following.

DEALING WITH DOWLING

It was at the man's suggestion that he and Miss Smy walk for a while up Fulham Road and at a slow pace so as not to attract any attention. He was shorter than Smy, perhaps 5 feet 8 inches in height and although a little overweight, moved nimbly enough. Smy guessed that he was probably in his mid-forties and noticed a small scar beneath his left eye. Upon introducing himself to Smy in the station entrance, he had removed his hat revealing a balding pate that gave him the appearance of a monk on a short vacation. Although he spoke in an easy manner, she strongly suspected that it covered a much more ruthless, even sinister, personality.

"May's a funny month, don't you find? One can never be sure how to dress. I'm glad I have my coat on now but it was a little warm to be wearing it this morning."

"Who are you?"

"Who am I? I am someone who has something in common with you, you'll be surprised to hear."

Smy looked sideways at him once more, determined to remain composed even though she was unnerved by the situation. "Something in common? Have we met before?"

"No, but we have both served the same employer. Tell me, how do you know Miss Armscott?"

"Are you from the police?"

"In a way. But I would be grateful if you would answer my question."

"Not until I know who you are."

"It might be better to begin by me telling you who you are. You are Winifred Smy. You live in Kenton, a small village in Suffolk. You were born in 1870, your father served and died in the army - Maiwand Pass I think - and your mother supplemented her pension working as a rush mat weaver for an employer in Debenham. In 1890 you came to London and eventually found a position as Governess with Lord Kenilworth. Whilst in that occupation you were approached by the Naval Intelligence Department and asked to execute a sensitive assignment on behalf of His Majesty's Government. How am I doing so far?"

"Her Majesty's Government, as it remained until 1901."

"You are right, but let me continue. Lord Kenilworth had a long-standing friendship with Alfred Von Tirpitz who, at that time, was chief of the German naval staff and about to present his recommendations to the Kaiser of how to strengthen the German fleet. Tirpitz, always eager to know just how much the British knew of his strategy, invited Lord Kenilworth and his family to Germany for four weeks. After an intensive German language course, your objective during your stay was, without Lord Kenilworth knowing, to inveigle yourself with any connection that you might find and to report it back to your superior, Sir Hector Butley-Low. It was, I have heard, a most detailed and constructive report. Knowing how the Germans were planning to strengthen their navy and the tactics Tirpitz was considering have been vital to our preparations for this war. You have already served this country with distinction."

Smy's mind was racing and the casual glances she threw from one side of the Fulham Road to the other were attempts to disguise the tumult of emotions she was feeling. "It is a strange sensation to have my past arrayed before me like this."

"I do so only to convince you that we are on the same side and serving the same purpose. Unless your sense of patriotism and duty has lessened in the intervening years, then we must trust one another implicitly."

"If we are to agree that," Smy threw back, "Then I really do need to know who you are and where you're from."

"Dowling, Secret Service Bureau, although it is more commonly known by its initials. It was formed six or seven years ago. Your chaps..."

"Chaps?"

"Oh, quite. Your people were subsumed into it along with other small departments. There's a nice café across the road there," Dowling nodded ahead. "Let's find a quiet table and share a pot of tea."

The cafe was not only warm but, sitting in the far corner as they were, Smy found it hard to imagine that one of London's busy streets was immediately outside. From where she sat, there were no raps of horses' hooves, rumble of tyres or the sound of people's footsteps on the pavement. As she waited for Dowling to join her, she watched an open-top bus glide silently past a small side window.

"Tea will soon be here," said Dowling, removing his coat and draping it over his chair. "Would have preferred a pint but all these new opening hours have stymied that. Now, let me repeat my question. Miss Armscott. How d'you know her?"

"I haven't met Miss Armscott but I have met Marguerite de

Gruchy."

"Ah, that's what she called herself was it? In The Goring; were you taken in by her disguise?"

"No, but she doesn't know that. Miss de Gruchy claimed that our Miss Armscott was a go-between and that any information meant for Miss de Gruchy should go via her."

Dowling took in the information before responding. "De Gruchy, eh? That's a new one. So why were you together at The Goring? With respect, I don't quite see where you fit in."

"She invited me. Here…" Smy took out the original letter that she had been sent.

Dowling reached inside his jacket pocket and took out his glasses. "Very posh. Can I keep this?"

"I can hardly refuse. So what is her real name?"

"Oh, it's Armscott, all right. So what was the thing she wanted to tell you? This 'certain information' she mentions."

At that moment, Smy froze with indecision. Where was all this leading? If she were to tell Dowling about Armscott's link with Laurie Morrie, what would the repercussions be? She suddenly felt that events were quickly racing away with her: the murder of the unknown man in the Assembly Hall; Spurling's untimely and suspicious death; the summoning by an unknown woman who told her that she was supposedly going to marry Laurie Morrie, a man she still suspected of framing her for the first death in Framlingham. No, this was all too fast and she was becoming giddy as question followed question. She must stall, she decided, not knowing whether that decision might also lead to an unfortunate end.

"Ah, here's the tea. Sugar, Mr Dowling?"

"Two please. Thank you."

"The great frustration for me was that Miss de Gruchy - as

she called herself - didn't seem to have anything to tell me. Very recently, in Framlingham, an unknown man was killed and I was, I'm afraid, their chief suspect. I had hoped that the meeting with Miss de Gruchy, whom I now know to be Miss Armscott, would yield the man's identity."

"But why go to you? Why not the police? And why would she take an interest in some murder in an East Anglian backwater? Doesn't make sense to me, Miss Smy."

"Nor to me. But when I was followed by your colleague as I left the hotel, I knew that there was something intriguing going on. I wondered if there was a connection with the Framlingham murder and that was why I wanted to meet our Miss Armscott."

Dowling sat back in his chair and scrutinised Smy over the rim of his cup. Had she thrown him off the scent? She couldn't be sure and, after all, she knew that men like Mr Dowling had been trained to receive information whilst preserving a perfectly blank expression.

"When did you know that I was following you, Mr Dowling? I was rather disappointed to have been so easily discovered."

"Compact mirror. Caught the sun for a moment and watched you for a while. Recognised you from the hotel, but my job at The Goring was to follow your dining companion, not you. You waiting outside the Admiralty this morning was too much of a coincidence. But I guessed you'd probably recognised me and knew what I was up to by then. So I couldn't change my plan. I was hoping that you'd approach Miss Armscott once we had got out at Walham Green station, but you didn't and so there was no use losing you both."

"Did you see what happened after you left?"

"Yes, I saw you go up to the house. Speak to the landlady,

did you? And I bet she told you that you were wrong and there was no one of that name living in her house. Lying, of course. Armscott lives there all right. She's probably given her landlady a bleeding heart story about a jealous boyfriend. You're not drinking your tea, Miss Smy."

"No, I seem to have drunk a lot of tea today. Well, what next, Mr Dowling?"

Dowling leant forward on the table and half-whispered, "What next will be your good self telling me the real information that Miss de Gruchy shared with you over lunch. Do I make myself clear?"

A STAGE-DOOR JOHNNY

"Miss Clemence not with you?"

"Well, as I did explain…"

Smy gently shook her head and turned back to the piano. "This is a lovely instrument. Broadwood. It has a big sound as well. Needs it in this hall. Oh, did you get the score I sent?"

"I did, thank you. So who's this Carreño? Obviously not English."

"Venezuelan." Smy rippled a scale over two octaves. "It's a lovely piece. Have you had a go at it?"

Tranmer carefully placed his violin case on a chair and unlocked the clasps. "I have. It's a nice thing but don't expect too much of me, especially the change in the middle to F sharp. To be honest, I haven't had much time to practise."

"Maud taking your life over, Herbert?"

Tranmer chose not to answer and placed the violin between his neck and shoulder. "If I could have an A please, Winifred."

Smy played the note and listened as it spun around the walls of the hall. She then placed her hands in her lap, waiting for Tranmer to tune the remaining strings. After a few seconds the steady pulse of the waltz was filling the space and, as they played, Tranmer and Smy exchanged occasional glances. Although she often enjoyed her time alone at her own piano, it was these moments of musical sharing that lifted her spirit the most.

Once they had completed the first awkward run-through, Tranmer turned away to practise the fingering of a particular passage he'd struggled with. Smy sat patiently at her piano and turned the sheets of the score over. The second playing of the piece was much more successful and this time their glances were often accompanied by a series of fleeting, satisfied smiles.

Just as the last notes of the music were ebbing away, Tranmer announced, "I have some news for you. Has Sibley been in contact?"

"No. What news?"

Tranmer sat down again and inspected the back of his violin. "They've found who your mysterious man was."

Smy immediately stood up. "What? You've been sitting there all this time and are only now telling me who it was!"

His teasing grin told Smy that she was being toyed with. "Tell me, Herbert, tell me who this man was."

"OK, but you're going to be disappointed."

"Why ever would I be disappointed?"

"Because he won't be of any help in your grand theories." Tranmer placed his violin carefully on a neighbouring chair and sat back. "His name is Ventnor. Horace Ventnor. A stage-door Johnny who was smitten with some London actress or other. Why he was with our Mr Wright that evening, I've no idea. Sad really, but there you have it."

"Wouldn't it be helpful to know who the actress was? That might go some way in telling us why he was in Framlingham."

"I haven't the time, Winifred. As I keep saying, this murder is Sibley's show. To be honest, he didn't seem to think it worth pursuing. His latest theory is that the woman that shot Ventnor was some jealous mistress who thought she was shooting Wright. Then, when she realised that she'd shot the wrong man, panicked and planted the gun on you when you burst into the room."

"But that doesn't add up. That gun was expertly passed into my pocket. And it would take a singular presence of mind to do such a thing so professionally."

"I'm only telling you what he told me. And I shouldn't be telling you that. Anyway, what's the real reason for our meeting here? We normally play our music together at your house. Other than it's a nice piano, there must be some rationale behind our change of venue?"

"There is. I will explain why in good time, but I need to share some thoughts with you first."

"Then it's a good job that Maud didn't come after all."

"To be perfectly honest, I was hoping she wouldn't. Anyway, my intuition tells me that she doesn't care much for me."

Tranmer seemed surprised by Smy's statement. "Well, she's never said anything like that to me."

"She will in time, believe me. I think she finds our friendship difficult to accept. But let's not get sidetracked. That first night in Framlingham, when this…Mr Ventor?"

"Ventnor."

"When this Mr Ventnor was murdered. I'd like to talk you through it. You'll need to use your imagination I'm afraid, so do pay attention."

Smy stood up and moved to the middle of the empty hall. "The stage - such as it was - was over there along that back wall. The orchestra, led by our Mr Spurling, was here. And the audience seating went from this point to the back of the hall. An aisle, which was round about here, split the audience into two blocks." Smy indicated these items of the room layout with a casual waving and pointing of her right arm.

"I'm with you. And I take it the dressing rooms were through that door at the side of the stage?"

"Exactly."

Smy clasped her hands, prayer-like, in front of her face and walked with slow steps towards the middle of the room. "At approximately 8.45 pm, Alfred Carver, Laurie Morrie's manager, approached me and said that Morrie had something to tell me. He also suggested I wait five minutes before going to his room."

"And did you wait?"

Smy nodded, her hands still held in front of her face. "Follow me please, Herbert. So I walked over to that door…"

Tranmer dutifully followed as Smy walked across the hall, through the door and into a square lobby with doors leading off into several rooms.

"…and this space was filled with people. Some of them were the performers that we'd seen, there were dogs from one of the acts running in and out and a general chaos everywhere. I then went up to Morrie's dressing room door and knocked like this." Smy rapped the same signal, two knocks followed by three more, that she'd used on that fateful night.

"What is that? Some sort of code?"

"Exactly that. He's always used it so as not to admit anyone he didn't know."

"And then you heard the gunshot?"

Smy ignored Tranmer's question and opened the door to enter the now-familiar room. "I walked in and was vaguely conscious of someone bumping into me and then…"

"And then?"

"Well, the door behind me was still open and everyone just filled the area around me. Next, stupidly, I pulled out a gun from my pocket."

"Exactly where was the man who'd been shot?"

Smy walked over to where the improvised dressing table had been. "Here. He was slumped over the desk, his face turned away. The strange thing is, there was nothing about him to suggest that it wasn't Laurie Morrie. He was even wearing the same silly sailor costume."

Tranmer rubbed his chin and looked around the room. "Sibley said that this Ventnor was obsessed with one particular actress. Hung around the stage door hoping for a word or something with her after her performances. Perhaps she was the killer. Got fed up of being pursued by this man and so colluded with Morrie and Carver to deal with him?"

Smy looked doubtful. "It all seems too elaborate to me. And why do such a thing in Framlingham of all places? London is a far better place to hide a murder."

"So when did this Morrie and Carver disappear? You'd seen Carver in the hall when you spoke to him, and people saw Morrie return to his dressing room after the performance."

"Oh, I've worked out that puzzle already, thanks to something Charlie Nunn let drop. Let's go outside." Smy led Tranmer back through the hall and out of the front of the building. They then walked around to the rear of the Assembly Hall, carefully navigating the weeds that the warmth of late spring had drawn into blossom.

"That wall is the back of the dressing room we've just been in. What do you notice?"

Tranmer, hands in pockets looked carefully, before replying, "It's a wall. What's there to notice?"

"Look again, carefully."

Tranmer walked closer, slightly annoyed at Smy's request. "It's still a wall. With a bricked-up door. Ah, wait a minute…"

"Wait a minute indeed. And when do you think they bricked the door up?"

"That I wouldn't know. But I presume you're about to tell me that it was very soon after the shooting of Ventnor."

"And so it was. It led, as you can see for yourself, straight into the dressing room that Laurie Morrie was using. Strange also that the back wall of the dressing room was decorated at the same time. All traces of the door on the inside have disappeared."

"Coincidence?" offered Tranmer.

"Maybe, but there's one other factor that suggests not. When you have a moment in your very busy romantic schedule, ask Inspector Sibley to inspect the wardrobe that belonged to Mr Spurling. I think he'll find it of some considerable interest."

Tranmer looked quizzically back at Smy. "Spurling's wardrobe? What about it?"

But Smy was walking back around the building and soon was out on Church Street again. Tranmer eventually caught up with her and was just about to repeat his wardrobe question when Charlie Nunn emerged from the entrance with a mop and pail in hand.

"Just the man!"

"Oh, hello Miss Smy. Everythin' set up for you OK this mornen? Ah, you as well, Inspector. Didn't see you there."

Smy cut in before Tranmer had a chance to respond. "Tell me, Charlie. The decorating that was done. Whose decision was that?"

"Decoratin'? Town Council, I suppose. Mr Spurling

complained about the draught in the room and said he'd almost caught his death in there when examinen the children with their playin'. Apparently someone on the council told 'im there were no funds but ol' Spurling said a kind benefactor would offer to pay for it. So all o' the bill went to this man via Spurling's address."

"Do you remember the man's name? The one that paid for everything."

"Course, I do, Miss Smy. Sent enough bills o'er to 'im. It were a Mr Dowling."

THE VENTING OF MRS VENTNOR

The revelation that Dowling, the Secret Service Bureau officer, might be the very same Dowling who had paid for the redecoration of the dressing room in which Ventnor had been shot, deeply concerned Winifred Smy. When Charlie Nunn had revealed Dowling's involvement, she had said nothing to Tranmer. He would have wanted to know how she knew Dowling, and that might have then led on to her employment many years ago with the Secret Service Bureau. No, she decided, for the time being at least, she would keep her link with Dowling to herself.

Her mind then turned back to the events in the Assembly Hall and she considered them in sequence. A famous music hall performer, Laurie Morrie, previously known to Smy, had agreed to do two performances on successive nights. An unknown drummer appears in the makeshift band who were to accompany Morrie and the other acts. Carver had asked her to go to Morrie's dressing room saying that Morrie had something he would like to tell her. She had done as Carver requested only to find that, moments before she entered the room, a shot was fired and Spurling's drummer had been shot in the back. And whilst Smy had entered the room and looked in astonishment at the murdered man, the killer had slipped the murder weapon into her pocket.

And what has she learned since? That Morrie, Carver and the killer had all disappeared. According to what Tranmer had learned, no one who was interviewed by the police could recall seeing any of them leave. Another nagging doubt that worked away in her brain was to do with Morrie and Carver. Why did they go to such lengths to make it look like Smy had been the killer? Yes, she had had her differences with Morrie many years ago, but to frame her for Ventnor's murder seemed cruelly disproportionate.

So now she had two mysteries to fathom: the Framlingham killings and the elusive Miss Armscott. There were two links to both: Morrie, and now Dowling. As Smy's mind could only function in a purely rational way, she had decided to suspend all possible theories and to go in search of facts. That was why she was now walking through the busy Framlingham market making for The Crown Hotel. It stood long and imposing along the top of the wide market square, a handsome two-storied building with a central carriageway at its centre. Above the upper windows in bold letters could be read, 'Commercial and Family Hotel and Posting House'.

As Smy entered the large oak-panelled room she noticed, to her satisfaction, that it was quite empty. She had deliberately chosen to arrive in mid-morning hoping that most guests would have either already checked out or been occupied somewhere in the town. A good fire was crackling and spitting in the large fireplace and, noticing the fresh logs on it, she assumed that it had only recently been tended to. A small desk just off the main area bore all of the accoutrements of a reception area: a bell to attract attention, a large letter desk blotter with a pen carefully arranged upon it, a desk paper spike with a collection of neatly skewered bills and - what she had really come for - the hotel guest register.

Smy looked around once more. She could hear someone was nearby but was finding it hard to locate exactly where the shuffling was coming from. Was it the nearby room that had a door slightly ajar? She went up to the counter, swivelled the register quickly so that it faced her and started to look for the most recent entries. A cloth ribbon made this part easy; now she just needed to work back to the dates that, if they had indeed stayed at this hotel as Carver's letter had originally informed her, Morrie and Carver would have registered their names.

Carver's letter had said that they would be arriving on the day of the first performance and, indeed, there were their two names booking two rooms for…one night. This confused Smy. Weren't there supposed to be two performances on the two successive nights? If that was so, then why had they booked to stay only the one evening? But that was not the only surprise Smy encountered. Looking further down the page was another entry for a 'Mr Horace Ventnor' although his entry showed that he was intending to stay for two nights. This fact caused Winifred Smy to stare in some confusion at the register and, whilst doing so, she failed to hear approaching footsteps.

"Can I ask you what you think you are doing?"

Smy looked around to see a rather tall, middle-aged man with a beautifully kept large moustache staring at her.

"I need to know if he was staying here or not."

"Staying here? Who was staying here?"

"My husband! With that woman!"

The man looked warily at Smy, not entirely sure what to say next. "Am I given to understand that you believe your husband has been a guest of ours, but was entertaining…other female company?"

"He's treated me like a fool. But I have nothing to prove that he has been having liaisons with her. I wanted to see if he'd stayed at your hotel."

"And you are?"

"Mrs Ventnor. Look here he is! Here is my husband. April the twenty-third. Why, of all the deceitful…"

The man was now beginning to feel uncomfortable with the situation that seemed to be unfolding and he stepped forward, saying in a discreet voice, "Mrs Ventnor, I can see that you are agitated. Please come into my office where we can talk about this more comfortably." His arm pointed Smy towards an adjoining room.

As Smy took her seat, the man closed the room door and walked behind a large desk and sat down. He gave a reassuring smile and said, "My name is Sewell. I am the manager of this hotel. If there is something you wish to find out then you have only to ask. The register is not for public perusal, as I'm sure you'll understand. Now, you expressed a concern about your husband's fidelity. A Mr Ventnor I think you said?"

"That's right. Horace Ventnor. I won't waste your time. I know you're busy and all, but it would be a blessing if I had some hard evidence that he's been seeing that awful woman." Smy could feel that, in her initial panic, she had chosen to speak with an accent that was part-Essex and part-Bow Bells, and was regretting not using her normal speaking voice for the duration of her theatrics.

Sewell walked back to the door, opened it and shouted, "Miss Day!" He looked downwards for a while until he was assured by approaching footsteps and rejoined Miss Smy.

"You need to see me, Mr Sewell?"

"Indeed. You were in reception on the 23rd April? I think it was the night we were welcoming our famous guest?"

Miss Day stood scarecrow-thin, her hands joined in such a way that Smy half-expected her to break into an operatic aria at any moment. Her long, greying hair was skillfully wound into a tight bun that sat behind her head. "Well, that's not a night that any of us will forget, certainly."

"Besides our honoured guest, do you recall another man staying with us by the name of Ventnor?"

"Horace Ventnor," added Smy.

"Why, yes. He registered in the afternoon, I recall."

"And, if you are able to also remember, was he accompanied by anyone?"

"What do you mean, 'accompanied'? He registered no one but himself. I could go and get the register for you…"

Sewell held up his hand, saying, "That won't be necessary. Mrs Ventnor, I think we have reassured you as much as we possibly can."

But Miss Day broke in once more. "If you'll forgive me for saying so, Mr Sewell, there was something that struck me as rather odd at the time. First, he insisted on paying for both nights in advance. But then he never returned to his room at all. Oh, and there was something else that was most unorthodox."

"Yes?"

"When the cleaner entered to service his room after the first night, all his belongings had disappeared. As if he had never been there at all."

Sewell rubbed his face with some concern. "Are you sure? Perhaps he came in during the day to collect his things and no one had noticed him?"

"I asked Boots…"

"Boots is our general handyman, Mrs Ventnor," Sewell interjected.

"I asked Boots whether he had been in the hotel at all since he left the first morning, and he told me that he'd only seen Mr Ventnor on the afternoon that he'd arrived when he smoked a whiff out in the yard. He'd asked Boots what time dinner was to be served but no one recalled seeing him at all after that."

"Well, Mrs Ventnor," said Sewell with a forced cheeriness. "I don't think we can help you any more than that."

Smy stood up and smiled at them both. "Oh no, let me tell you that this has been a most enlightening conversation."

THE MISERY OF MANNERS

In a little over three-quarters of an hour since leaving The Crown Hotel, Smy found herself cycling past Kenton's more modest coronet: The Crown pub. And it was there that she saw a very disconsolate-looking Nigel Manners who had taken one of the bar stools outside and was now nursing an almost-drained tankard of beer.

"Mr Manners?"

"Oh, Miss Smy…I called on you earlier. I…oh, excuse me, would you like a drink?"

"I'm fine, thank you. To be honest, I was looking forward to making a pot of tea."

Manners quickly drained his glass, most of the contents of which now slid down the outside of his face and inside his shirt collar. "Tea would be lovely."

Smy hadn't been contemplating company when she had informed Manners of her intention, but she dismounted her bicycle and waited whilst Manners returned the glass and barstool to the bar. She noticed that, as he re-emerged from the pub, there seemed a heaviness about him that was singularly uncharacteristic. She had become so used to his unquenchable enthusiasm, often betrayed by the nervy twitching and stabbing of his pipe-cleaner limbs, that she found herself feeling genuinely sympathetic towards him.

"I'm sorry I was out. I've just been to Framlingham. If I'd known you wanted to see me…"

"Oh, yes, that would have…" but Manners, so distracted by the churning of his thoughts, failed to finish his sentence. Smy thought that she would wait for Manners to speak, deciding that he might be carefully preparing what he wanted to say. Whatever it was, it was obviously troubling him. Silently, they entered the village, Smy saying nothing but a pleasant 'hello' to Lily Lambert, her tiny barefoot frame encased in a long thin dress, who was drawing water from the water pump that stood slightly back from the road.

On reaching the house, Manners had still not said anything and it occurred to Smy that the matter troubling him might be unconnected with the recent happenings in Framlingham and were, perhaps, of a more romantic origin. This, she decided, should be her entry point for the discussion.

"How is your fiancée, Miss Bartholomew? I hope she's keeping well."

Manners jerked his head up to answer. "Oh, Beatrice? She's…she's fine."

Smy continued to make the tea as another silence descended. Remembering Manners' fondness for cake, she placed the tea tray on the table together with a generous slice of seed cake. "Milk and sugar?" she asked.

"Yes, to both. Three sugars. My goodness, is that a slice of seed cake?" A twitch of animation was immediately evident in Manners' face as he asked.

"Help yourself. Let me know if you'd like another slice."

Smy's ruse worked perfectly: Manners soon alternating between mouthfuls of cake and sips of tea. Nevertheless, he still had a troubled look about him.

"You don't seem like your old self, Mr Manners."

The question caused Manners to momentarily halt his cake consumption. "I am…I am defeated. That's the long and short of it, Miss Smy. Utterly defeated."

"Another slice?"

"Would you mind? It was a long walk."

"From Framlingham?"

"Well, not quite. I managed to cadge a lift to The Crown. I meant a long walk from there to your house."

"So what is it that's defeated you?"

"Not what, but whom. My beastly editor. I just don't understand him. It's as if he wants me to fail. Perhaps it's time to move on from Framlingham. Find myself another paper. This cake is wonderful, Miss Smy. Here, could I trouble you for…"

"Do have another slice. I'll wrap some up later for you to take home. But what's happened with your editor?"

Manners dabbed the tip of his finger on his tongue and then started to stab at the remaining crumbs on his plate. "It's this shooting business. Apparently the murdered man was called Ventnor. Stories like that shooting come once in a lifetime when you're working on a provincial newspaper. And then there's Laurie Morrie's disappearance as well, not to mention old Spurling, the music man. Happenings such as these are like hen's teeth to a journalist, Miss Smy, hen's teeth."

'So what's the problem? You're covering both killings, aren't you?"

But Manners shook his head slowly at Smy. "That's just it. My editor has told me to concentrate on other things. To put it aside, that's what he said, forget they ever happened. Two of the biggest stories to land in my lap and I'm told to forget they ever happened!"

Smy was about to remind Manners of the other 'events' that they had worked on together, but concluded that now was not the time. "Did he tell you why?"

"Not a single word of explanation. Called me into his office. Told me that there were developments that were taking place and that someone from on high had asked the paper to keep its distance."

"And who was this someone who asked him? Did he tell you?"

"You have to understand that my editor has a look. A 'there's-what-I-wanted-to-tell-you-now-go-away' type of look. When he gives you that look, you don't ask why."

Smy felt genuinely sorry for Manners. It had been four years since they had first joined forces on the Kenton Junction murder, and a grudging admiration of Manners' gifts - although often hidden beneath a patronising and thoughtless manner - had grown within Miss Smy.

"Have you any theories as to why he asked you to step away from those stories?"

"I have racked my brains over and over about it. Did I not report it correctly? Did I go beyond my responsibilities to the readership? I'm at a loss! I'm quite devastated by it. It's quite simply the end of the world. A professional disaster from which I doubt I shall ever recover. I say, is there more tea in that pot? I've an awful thirst."

As Smy poured, Manners slumped once more into his chair.

"Mr Manners, in the past you and I have worked well together. And I have come to value your talents. If you were to reassure me that the conversation I would like to share with you would remain between us, then I think we may embark on another mutually profitable venture."

Manners sat up as if demonstrating the reaction of the very first frog's leg that had been stimulated by the knife of Galvani's wife. "What would it take for me to reassure you? You know that my word…"

"Is not always your bond, but I must admit that you have never failed me yet." Smy moved the tea tray to the far end of the kitchen table and looked deeply into the eyes of Manners.

"They shot the wrong man. The man they intended to kill was Laurie Morrie, not Horace Ventnor. Inspector Sibley apparently believes it was…"

"It was a jealous lover, or something."

"That's right. But I don't think that was true. It was all too elaborate, and I am certain that both Morrie and Carver, his manager, were in on it. Why else disappear? And why arrange for Mr Ventnor to sit at Morrie's dressing room table? Morrie was fiercely protective of any dressing room he was in. He even used to have a code if you wanted to enter because he loathed meeting people after a performance."

"Inspector Sibley told me that they first suspected you, that you shot this man thinking it was Morrie. Then he changed his tune and said that it was some woman and that you just happened to be in the wrong place at the wrong time."

"The Inspector is half right. I didn't shoot Ventnor, but things had been carefully arranged to make it look like it was me who'd shot him."

"Why, Miss Smy? I don't understand. Why would Morrie do such a thing?"

"I'm not sure, but one thing that I want to tell you - and this must never leave this room - is that I fell out with Morrie many years ago. You see, I first met him in London when I was just twenty years of age. I'd just started working as a Governess."

"You fell out? Over what?"

"That I can't tell you and it's not relevant to this discussion, Mr Manners."

Manners sprang out of his chair, his limbs gradually jerking and flexing as of old. "You're telling me that the person they meant to shoot was Morrie? It's…it's unbelievable."

"Maybe so, but everyone was convinced it was Morrie that had been shot right up to the point where I had to identify him."

"But surely it was obvious that…"

"That's just it. Even I thought it was Morrie when I went into that room. He was slumped over the same table that I had seen him sitting at in the interval that same night. He even had the same clothes on. His hair had been slicked down just as Morrie's had been for the night's performance. The make-up and everything was so well done that even I was fooled."

Manners sat down again. "The poor man. Apparently he was the drummer in Spurling's little orchestra. To die…hang on. So how did the other two, this Carver chap and Morrie disappear?"

"You're not going to believe me."

"My sense of credulity has already been most severely tested. Try me."

"I don't think either of them ever went back into that dressing room once the show was over. I'm convinced now that once Carver had instructed me to go to Morrie's dressing room, he then left the building. Morrie, I am certain, left immediately after he left the stage."

"But what about this woman who supposedly shot Ventnor?

Where did she disappear to?"

"Ah, well that, Mr Manners, is where you come in."

FINDING MISS WRIGHT

Smy couldn't remember the last time that she had felt so agitated or confused. It was, she concluded, a completely illogical act to have done. Why had she not followed her head instead of allowing her emotions to sway her decision? But the damage was done and here she was in Langham Place, London, pacing the pavement outside the Queen's Hall.

Questions tumbled persistently through her mind. Perhaps she won't have received the letter? Maybe she was away when it arrived? It may never have reached her because the post room of the hall would think it an impertinence to send a personal letter… 'Stop it!' she told herself, trying to halt her descent into the maddening doubts that were slowly engulfing her. She resolved to stand still and concentrate instead on the busy traffic passing before her.

"Win?"

She knew the voice, even though the passage of years had been so long. A soft-spoken voice sounding like an echo from a long-distant scene. She turned slowly and there before her stood Eleanor Wright. The hair had lost some of the deep lustre that had shone whenever sunlight glanced across it, and though the youthful freshness of her skin had given way to inevitable age, Smy was still struck by her loveliness.

"Eleanor, I thought you might not come. My letter…it was such a silly thing, but I had no address for you."

"It was passed on to me. It's been a very long time. You're looking so well. How are you?"

Smy felt a lock of her own hair fall across her face, which she nervously swept back into place. "I am well. And you look so well! What's your secret?"

Eleanor Wright laughed and, as she did so, the tension dissolved a little between them. Smy looked around quickly. Since her last experience with Dowling, she had grown very wary of being watched and was alert to others maybe doing so since she had alighted at Liverpool Street Station.

"Thank you for seeing me. How long do you have?"

"We've broken for an early lunch. Probably an hour at best. Been rehearsing all morning actually. Speyer's a bit of a martinet but I like him. I don't know how he carries on with all these terrible things people are saying about him. I even heard he'd been accused of signalling to German submarines from his house!"

"Now every German's a bad German, it seems. Is there somewhere we can talk? I'd kill for a cup of tea."

They walked to a small café nearby that Eleanor suggested and ordered some sandwiches. Once the waitress had taken their order, they found that the same awkwardness had returned.

"It's nice talking to someone other than a policeman, Win."

"Have they been able to tell you anything?"

"About Lawrence? No. Wasn't it near where you live, this shooting?"

"Framlingham. It's a little town. It was supposed to be a charity concert. I was there."

"Did you…did you see Lawrence at all?"

"Briefly."

Eleanor suddenly leaned forward, the table wobbling momentarily as she did so. "It's been a long time, Win. I've been trying to remember the name of that dreadful place you first stayed in?"

"When I first came to London? I don't know if it had a name. It was on Crispin Street. You're right, it was truly terrible. I was desperate. I needed somewhere."

The tea and sandwiches arrived and they assisted the waitress in laying the various plates onto the table.

"It's all so long ago now, isn't it? Was it twenty years ago?"

"More like twenty-five. Do you remember the flat I moved to next? It was in that little room over the shop on Union Street."

"Cosy. Small and cosy. But now you're back in Suffolk again?" Eleanor poured the tea and offered Smy a sandwich.

Putting the sandwich aside, Smy took the plunge and related - as unemotionally as she could - all that had happened in Framlingham, although she excluded the planting of the gun, unsure if such a detail was necessary. Eleanor's face was set firm, reflecting the same lack of emotion although small nods and movements of her head betrayed the depth of feeling about all that had happened.

"You know I've not seen Lawrence for many years. He never forgave either of us. Knowing Lawrence, he never will. His darling little sister in prison. Whatever next?"

"And we still haven't got the vote. I've often wondered if all the pain was worth it. What with the war and everything, the cause seems as far away as it ever was."

"I will never forgive myself for persuading you to…"

Eleanor Wright held up her hand, her face suddenly becoming troubled. "I prefer not to think about it. That prison, those awful people. Please, Win, don't let's talk about it." Eleanor watched as her hand slowly stirred the spoon in her teacup whilst Smy silently berated herself for having brought the subject up. Still watching the circular path of her spoon, Eleanor asked, "Did you ever marry? Have you a nice man back in Suffolk? I was never sure if you were the marrying kind."

Smy shook her head. "I'm firmly on the road to becoming an old maid. No husband. No children. A truculent, difficult old maid. And you?"

A rather large woman leaving a neighbouring table lost her balance a little and brushed against their table, causing it to wobble once more. "I'm sorry. Silly me."

"Nothing broken," said Smy. The woman apologised again and made her way to the front of the café.

"I hear that Lawrence has a new lady in his life. A Miss Armscott. Did you know?"

"No, I didn't know. Well, whoever she is, she'll be the latest in a long line of women for our poor Lawrence. Not the committed type, my brother. To be honest, Win, Lawrence and I are long past caring for each other. As you'll remember, it was never 'happy families' in the Wright household. Is he still hanging around with that slimy dresser?"

"Carver? Yes. As thick as thieves as they ever were. Does he live with Lawrence?"

Eleanor thought for a moment. "Well, I don't think so. Like I said, it's so long since I saw either of them. I thought Carver lived out Fulham way. Used to have a little flat in some large old house, I think."

"Eleanor, I'd like to see Lawrence. To be honest, I have something I need to ask him."

"You're going to ask me where Lawrence is, aren't you? Was that the only reason you wanted to see me? Because if it was, then you've made a fruitless journey. The police seem to think I know where he is as well. Well, I don't. Sorry if that's a disappointment to you."

Smy pushed the sandwich away, knowing that she had no appetite for it. Once more, words eluded her. It was Eleanor who spoke again. "These sandwiches have seen better days. I suspect they've been on display since Christmas."

"You know, you're right, I thought you might know where Lawrence was and, to be honest, I could have had this conversation with you by mail. But the whole situation had brought back that time when we…when we left on bad terms. If you must know, I couldn't deny myself the chance to see you again."

Smy saw that Eleanor's eyes had become glassy and the two of them looked at each other until Smy, conscious of the other customers in the café, looked embarrassedly away.

"Win, as I said, I don't know where Lawrence is and I don't care where Lawrence is. But if I were you, I would ask myself where a man of his habits would hide? One other thing: he has changed very little since you last saw him. He had only one bolthole when you first met him and, to my knowledge, things haven't changed. You may not end up at the right place, but you'll not be far away."

"Gambling. Horses. Brighton?"

"I'm saying nothing. Now, I must be back. The orchestra is going to find the Brahms violin concerto rather awkward without their principal violinist." And it was then that Smy noticed something that she had failed to see all through their meeting: the wedding band on Eleanor's finger.

BRIGHTON BOUND

The conversation with Eleanor had forced Smy into a dilemma. Does she return to Suffolk and continue with her hunt for Ventnor and Spurling's killers, or does she journey on to Brighton to find Lawrence Wright and Alfred Carver - if that was where they indeed were - to confront them with their treatment of her in Framlingham? The problem that she had with the latter option was that she did not have a change of clothes, having originally intended being in London only for part of the day before returning to Suffolk. Nevertheless, she felt compelled to go to Brighton realising that Eleanor's hint of Lawrence's likely location was a credible one.

Smy first called into a bank and took out enough money to pay for accommodation. She then walked to the Bourne and Hollingsworth department store on Oxford Street and bought a change of blouse, undergarments and a favourite soap. As the day was cold but clear she chose to walk to Victoria Station, but made sure her route took her down Whitehall, determined to see if Dowling was still closely watching the comings and goings of Miss Armscott. But, as she walked past Admiralty House, Dowling was nowhere to be seen and neither was there another observer in his stead. As she carried on her way, Smy feigned to look through various shop windows, carefully scanning the reflections in case she had been assigned a new follower.

Knowing that she still needed to find somewhere to stay in Brighton, she pressed on for Victoria station and bought her train ticket. Once again, where she could, she kept to the sides of the building, always scanning the concourse for anyone who might be watching her. Having not eaten at lunchtime, she bought a cup of tea and a slice of ginger cake in a café just off the main area and looked on as people criss-crossed the large space, all bustling to or from their respective trains. A soldier sat on the concourse floor with his haversack next to him and lit a cigarette. A woman and her daughter anxiously scanned the arrival and departure boards. A drunk danced in circles but somehow managed to avoid colliding with the throng rushing around him.

Smy finished her cake and tea and walked quickly to her platform. Once on the train, she took out a newspaper she had bought earlier and leafed through it. Glancing at the passengers who were still walking down the platform to their carriages, she was astonished to see - unmistakably - Miss Armscott walking alongside the train. She held the paper up, confident that she hadn't been seen and, once she had passed her window, Smy took the opposite seat to see her open the door and board a neighbouring carriage.

It was then that she noticed Dowling sidle past her window. Even from the back, he was easily recognisable to her: the same deliberate steps and dark brown coat. Using her paper as a screen once more, she now turned her attention to the corridor hoping that he would not be joining her in her compartment. The door was suddenly yanked open and in stepped a rather weaselly-looking man, small in stature and with a rather timid manner.

"Good afternoon." He removed his hat and began to search his briefcase for his own paper. Smy fixed her attention back to the corridor, but all those that went past were, thankfully, people she didn't know.

Just as the train began to move away, the man opposite Smy looked at her shopping bags and asked, "An expensive day out, one fears?"

"Je suis vraiment désolée, je ne parle pas anglais."

Smy was dearly hoping that the man didn't speak French. Thankfully, he nodded embarrassedly and returned, "Oh, yes, and perhaps a little rain tomorrow," and continued reading his paper.

The train journey was the perfect time for Smy to think about where she would stay in Brighton. What was imperative was to remain incognito; if she could indeed locate Wright and Carver - preferably without the attentions of Dowling - then she would have the opportunity to confront them. She knew from old that when it came to staying anywhere, Lawrence Wright's instincts would fix firmly on the most expensive hotel available. But, Smy reasoned, as he was presumably in hiding, staying somewhere like The Grand in Brighton might be an obvious location for those who were in pursuit of him. No, she decided, he will have found somewhere more suited to 'laying low'. The depressing thought for Smy was that there were many hotels and sundry guesthouses in the Brighton area and it would be a long, uphill task trying to track down Wright and Carver's preferred accommodation.

When the train finally pulled into Brighton station, the man stood up, raised his hat at Miss Smy and left. Smy felt it would be better to wait until she was sure that both Miss Armscott and Dowling had left the train. She had worked out that their carriages must be closer to the station's exit gate, so gathered her things and walked to the back of the train, before stepping down onto the platform. It gave her a good view of the people who had alighted, many of whom were already walking past the engine. She tipped the brim of her hat slightly forward and walked slowly along the length of the platform. To her great relief, neither Armscott nor Dowling could be seen.

Smy walked over to a cheerful-looking railway porter who had tipped the peak of his cap at her and asked where she might be able to find a small hotel or guest house near the seafront. "You know, one that only local people might recommend."

"Well, I hear many good things about Mrs Walters' place on York Road. Very clean and an excellent breakfast, apparently."

"And that's in Brighton, is it?"

"Hove, actually. But as near as you can get to Brighton without actually being in it. It's only a twenty-minute walk, I reckon, easily."

The man drew some instructions for Smy on her newspaper and, on reaching the guest house, she was delighted to see that the porter had indeed recommended a very welcoming place for her to stay. Whilst Mrs Walters was obtaining the key, Smy glanced quickly through the register to make sure that the other five occupants did not include Dowling or Armscott.

Mrs Walters led Smy into her room and told her when the evening meal and breakfast would be served. "It's good, honest food we serve here. I hope it's to your liking."

"Oh, I'm sure it will be. Can I just ask if there are any races planned for tomorrow?"

"Races? Don't you know? They stopped all the races when the war broke out. I do hope you've not come to Brighton just for the races."

"Oh, I should have thought of that. Never mind. I'm sure I'll find plenty of other things to do. And is there a post office nearby? I'd like to send a telegram."

"Come back to reception and tell me what you want sent. Albert'll run it for you."

"Let me just unpack my things first and I'll be down."

Smy could tell that Mrs Walters was a little suspicious, but decided that the best thing to do was to brazen it out. She found a slip of paper and pen on the room's writing desk, and wrote: CHANGE OF PLAN STOP AM IN BRIGHTON STOP THINK LW IS HERE STOP REPLY THIS ADDRESS.

The telegram was addressed to Nigel Manners, and Albert - Mrs Walters' teenage son - hared away with the promise of a good tip from Smy.

She sat on the end of the bed and could see a sliver of blue sky above the neighbouring houses' chimneys. In her mind she turned over the fact that either tomorrow was going to be an important day - or she had set out on a fool's errand.

ROOM FORTY-NINE

It was a strong, unwelcoming wind that skimmed low from the sea, which slowly swelled and shrank like the green-grey torso of a somnolent dinosaur. Fortified by a good breakfast and wrapped in her coat, Smy walked along the seafront from Hove into Brighton. Always watchful of the crowd, she sauntered as casually as she could and, as Mrs Walters had remarked to her the previous evening at dinner, was struck by the presence of many Indian soldiers who were convalescing in The Royal Pavilion, their wounds sufficiently healed so that they could venture out and taste the sea-salt tang of the air.

One of the hotel residents, a sly man whom Smy had already taken a dislike to, had loudly expressed his displeasure of the Indian contingent that morning: "They've got no right to stay in the good King's building. No right at all. They ain't like us. They're dirty."

"And who would I rather stand by me to fight the Kaiser?" Smy had replied. "Brave Indian soldiers willing to die for our way of life, or an oily travelling salesman?"

Smy had left the room immediately after her barbed response, with the other resident momentarily lost for words, although she did hear him throw back, "Who the hell does she think she is? The little..." But, by the time Smy had reached the landing, his final words couldn't be heard.

Smy now pulled her coat tightly around her for warmth and decided to make for the labyrinth of small alleys and passages known locally as 'The Lanes'. Still remaining watchful, she threw furtive glances to left and right, knowing that there were now possibly four people who might see her first: Lawrence Wright, Miss Armscott, Alfred Carver and, perhaps the most worrying one of all, Dowling. As she entered Meeting House Lane she stepped quickly into the doorway of a butcher's shop, which provided an excellent view of the lane itself. Having satisfied herself that all was reasonably clear (after all, one of the four might emerge from any shop along the lane's length) she walked on, always eyeing those that she could see some way ahead.

She realised that she had been preoccupied with where Wright, Carver and Armscott might be staying, but had given no thought to Mr Dowling. Had he expected to find himself in Brighton? She remembered that he had no case with him as he trailed Miss Armscott along the platform at Victoria Station, so perhaps, like Smy, had to improvise accommodation when he'd reached Brighton.

Smy was beginning to doubt whether she had chosen the right way to locate Wright. After all, she could have interrogated the various hotel registers as she had done in Framlingham, but this would have had to be done in wide, open reception areas where she might be seen at any moment. She continued sidling through the lanes and small alleys before deciding that the hotel register - even with its attendant risks - might be the wiser option. She found herself walking southwards on Ship Street and turned right onto the coast road that would return her to Hove.

At the corner she noticed the Old Ship Hotel and, gathering her courage, entered and waited until a guest had left their key with the receptionist.

"Can I help, Madam?"

"I hope so. I'm looking for two members of my family. You see we're here for a wedding and I can't remember where they said they'd found accommodation."

"And their names?"

"Mr Wright and Mr Carver."

The man pulled the register towards him and flicked slowly through the pages. "Not that I can see. Are you sure it was this hotel?"

"Well, that's just it, I'm not sure myself. Anyway, you've been very helpful. Thank you."

Smy soon found herself back on the main coast road and, with the same cold wind sweeping icily across the seafront, she gripped her coat tight about her once more and walked back in the direction of her hotel.

It was when she was passing the impressive Georgian frontage of the Bedford Hotel that she experienced a somewhat bizarre encounter. A group of men had assembled outside on the pavement, taking a break from what appeared to be a large business meeting, and were now smoking their cigarettes and cigars. As Smy threaded her way through the group she noticed in the corner of her eye a small woman walking quickly from the canopied hotel entrance. The woman, who was in a rush to make her way through the crowd failed to notice Smy and brushed heavily against her. Both Smy and the woman stood back after the collision and looked at each other. The woman, who was carrying a small wicker basket with a scarf draped across it, smiled and hurried away.

Smy stood for some seconds trying to make sense of the encounter and then smelled the arm of her coat. The scent was unmistakable: a mixture of cheap perfume and a distinctive body odour. A worrying thought suddenly entered her mind and she rushed through the hotel entrance and immediately caught the attention of the concierge.

"Excuse me, I'm looking for my friends. They told me I would find them here. A Mr Wright…"

"I think you'd best ask reception. I wouldn't…"

Smy didn't wait but repeated the question to a woman behind the reception desk. The woman, who Smy noted had a rather self-satisfied and condescending manner, told her that there was no one staying at the hotel by that name.

"Perhaps you have a Mr Carver staying with you? A Mr Alfred Carver?"

"We do not, Madam. Are you sure that you are in the right hotel?"

Smy chose not to communicate the anger - mixed with a great anxiety - that was mounting within her. What names could they have used? She held her fingertips to her temples and thought, certain that this was the hotel in which they were staying. "Have you two friends staying whose names are Alfred and Lawrence?"

"I cannot say. We refer to our guests only by their last names."

"I know that. But this is very important, believe me. I would not be pressing you if it were not vital that I speak to them. Can you check your hotel register for me?"

"You're not seriously suggesting…"

But Smy's patience was now exhausted and she grabbed the register and took it into the neighbouring function room, swiftly turning over the pages. A shout for the concierge went up from the receptionist as she ran around to the front of the desk in pursuit of Smy, who was still furiously interrogating the pages of the register. And there it was: Mr Lawrence Marin. He couldn't deny himself the private joke of using the French word for a sailor as his invented surname.

The receptionist, in a state of high dudgeon, wrenched back the register from Smy. You really are most rude and I shall call the police. How dare you!"

"Mr Marin. What room?"

"What room? Who are you to ask such things? Do you seriously think I would pass on the details of our guests' rooms?"

Smy rushed back into the reception lounge and caught the eye of a hotel maid who was coming down the staircase carrying a tray.

"Excuse me, this is most important. A Mr Marin is staying here and I must speak to him right away. Do you know his room number?"

"His room number. Marin. The tall gentleman. Yes, what number is it now…"

"Please, please think hard."

"Forty-nine. Yes, that's it, number forty-nine."

But Smy was now bounding up the stairs, with the arrogant receptionist still chasing after her, looking at the brass plates at the head of each landing bearing the room numbers of that floor with an arrow indicating the direction. On the second floor she saw that rooms '40 - 58' were to her left and she now slowed down to a rapid walk following the room numbers on each door. The receptionist, in close attendance, was still berating her with a repetition of "What in heaven's name do you think you're doing?" and an occasional demand that the concierge catch up with them.

Smy was soon at the door to number forty-nine and she used the knocking signal that would let Wright know that there was someone outside that he could trust. But there was no answer, so she hurriedly repeated the signal. All that could be heard was the clomping footsteps of the angry receptionist, who was now out of breath and leaning with her back against the wall in an effort to recover herself.

Trying the handle, Smy found that the door was open and let herself in. But she knew instantly that she was too late. A table was in the middle of the room with two hands of cards face down on either side. Lawrence Wright was slumped back in his chair, his eyes eerily half-open and a large and bloody bullet wound staining the front of his shirt. Another man who had been facing Wright and also without a jacket, was slumped over the same table. And then Smy noticed the third body, lying on the carpet outside the door that led into the adjoining bathroom.

The receptionist, who had now caught her breath and followed Smy into the room, slowly took in the grim spectacle before her and gasped with her hand over her mouth. "My god, oh my god, oh my god!"

Smy calmly turned to her, "Get the manager and the police. Now! Quick!" The woman bumped into the concierge as she left the room, unable to find the words that would describe to him what she had just seen. Smy quickly took in the gruesome tableau and then saw that there was a gun in the unknown man's hand that lay on the table. It was, unmistakably, a Webley Mark VI service revolver.

MARKED CARDS

"You said you knew two of the dead men. Any next-of-kin?"

"I only know Mr Wright's family. A sister. Eleanor Wright."

"But not any of Mr Carver's family?"

"No, officer. I don't know anything about his family."

"Perhaps he was married?"

Smy shrugged. "I'd not seen either of them for twenty years or so. If Mr Carver had since gotten married, I wouldn't have been aware of it."

The police interviews were all taking place in a bedroom on the first floor of the Bedford Hotel. As Miss Smy and the receptionist were first on the scene, both were, in turn, being rigorously questioned by the sergeant.

"Were Mr Wright or Mr Carver expecting you?"

"No, it was a surprise call. I was in Brighton for a few days and Eleanor, Mr Wright's sister, told me that they were staying nearby."

The police sergeant, a large and imposing man whose girth was only just accommodated by his police tunic, wrote down the replies of Smy with a slowness that reminded her of an unacademic schoolboy. "Now Miss Smy, you said you didn't recognise the third man. Are you absolutely sure about that? He was lying with his face partly hidden. What if I was to arrange a proper view, might that help?"

"I saw enough to know that he wasn't someone I'd ever met before. I'm quite certain of that."

The sergeant placed down his pencil on his notebook and smiled at Miss Smy. "I think we're done for now. When were you planning to return home?"

"Tomorrow. It will take me a good part of the day, but the police station at Framlingham will know where to contact me should you have any more questions."

"I'm sorry that your visit to Brighton has been ruined for you. I'm afraid that altercations, violent ones like this, are fairly rare. But I suppose if people sit down to gamble at cards with guns in their pockets, then it sometimes doesn't take much for things to turn, what might we say, a bit ugly."

Smy was grateful for the opportunity to stand up again. "Are you saying that that was what happened? That there was a disagreement and it escalated into...well, what I discovered in the room?"

The sergeant stretched his arms wide, yawned and walked to the window. "Not such a good view, is it? I'd want my money back if this was the view I had. Just the back of a lot of buildings, and very unattractive ones at that. Disagreement? Well, that's what it looked like to me. Poker is a very emotional game, I hear. One accuses the other of cheating and, well, you don't need much imagination with what happens next."

"So you think they shot each other?"

"Of course. Stands to reason, really. One pulls out a gun and then the other pulls out a gun and..."

"Except that there was only one gun. If the man whom I didn't recognise shot Mr Wright and Mr Carver, then who shot him?"

The sergeant looked a little flustered for a moment. "Now don't you go worrying your lovely little head about that. I'm sure that all will be revealed once…"

"I'm not worrying my lovely little head at all, and would prefer that you didn't patronise my observations. I am confident that you'll not find any other gun in that room, Sergeant. What's more, I would stake my life on the fact that all three men were shot by the same gun."

"But there were only two bullets fired from the gun. There must have been another gun that killed this unknown man."

"That's exactly what they want you to believe. My conviction is that three bullets were fired from one gun and then an extra bullet was replaced in the chamber to lull you into that conclusion."

The sergeant picked up his notebook and pencil and opened the door for Smy. "Thank you for sharing your very imaginative thoughts, Miss Smy. You'll appreciate, I'm sure, that we have other people to speak to."

Smy arched an eyebrow at the policeman and put on her coat. "I know that you are quite decided in what may have happened in room forty-nine, but there are questions that I would like answered. For instance, why were the two hands of cards all face down in front of the two players? I can tell you that Wright was a five-card stud poker man. If there were five cards on the table then four cards would have been face up. How can two players possibly fall out over a card game if all five cards are face down?"

But the sergeant was now summoning over another officer who was standing in the hotel corridor. "Tomkins, take Miss Smy to the ground floor will you? Good man."

Smy, irritated with the dismissiveness of the police sergeant, waited for a moment under the canopy of the hotel entrance for her anger to abate. Ahead of her, the sea was heaving with a slow languor, with its rim on the horizon now almost indiscernible from the leaden sky. A few brave souls were walking along the water's edge and two or three couples huddled close on the benches that overlooked the sea. Glancing to her left, Miss Smy was astonished to see a figure leaving the West Pier whom she immediately recognised. Doing everything she could to avoid being seen until she was ready, Smy walked in a deliberately circuitous route towards her before saying cheerily, "Why, it's Miss de Gruchy!"

Miss de Gruchy was taken aback and it was a few moments before she could compose herself. "Excuse me…oh, Miss Smy. What a surprise. A very lovely surprise, of course. Are you on holiday?"

"Only a couple of days rest. Visiting old friends. It's a nice change from Suffolk."

"Why, yes, I'm sure it is."

Smy sensed that Miss de Gruchy - or Miss Armscott - was anxious to keep the meeting brief. "Where are you staying? We really must have tea together again."

"At the Bedford." She indicated the hotel with her umbrella. "It's very nice. Are you staying in Brighton as well?"

"Hove. A small guest house. Excellently run. Tell me, are you walking back to your hotel now?"

Once more, Miss de Gruchy was flailing for an answer. Eventually she nodded, "Yes. I do need to lie down for a few moments. The walk and the sea air…well, you know it tires one so when one is not used to it."

"May I have a discreet word?" Smy's voice lowered as she said this, something which de Gruchy did not fail to notice.

"A discreet word? What about?"

"Polly, I have some rather terrible news for you. Please listen to me, it's about Lawrence."

"Lawrence? What about Lawrence?"

"He's been shot. So has Alfred Carver."

Polly Armscott looked incredulously at Smy, unable to take in what she was being told. "Shot. Are you mad? Are you sure it was Alfred?"

Smy took Armscott by the arms and looked at her squarely in the face. "Quite sure. I recognised them both. The police are in the hotel at this very moment. They've just finished interviewing me."

"You? Why would they…"

"Because I walked into see Lawrence, in room forty-nine, and both Lawrence and Carver were dead."

All colour had completely drained from Armscott's face, her skin tone now a whitish-grey that matched the pale clouds overhead. "I think I'm going to be sick."

Smy directed her towards an empty bench and sat her down, her arm gripping the side of her seat for support. "This is all a terrible dream. I, I must be dreaming."

"You're not dreaming. What number is your room? I take it you were telling me the truth about staying at the Bedford?"

Armscott shook her head. "No, I'm at The Old Ship. I must have got confused."

"Of course, there was another man involved as well. I'm afraid he was also dead in Lawrence's room. You may know him."

"Know him? The only people I know here are…were Lawrence and Alfred. There isn't anyone else I know."

"Oh, I only mention it because he's been following you. He's been following you in London and was even on the same train that you came down on to Brighton."

"Following me. Someone's been following me?"

"I think you and I will have to stop pretending, Polly. No more Miss de Gruchy. I've known for some time who you really were. I'm not sure exactly what's been going on with you and Lawrence, but I think your life may be in great danger."

Polly Armscott drew out a handkerchief and wiped her eyes. "I don't know what you're talking about. Me being followed. Why would someone want to follow me? Who was this other man in the room?"

"I lied to the police and told them that I didn't recognise him, but I'm afraid I did know him. His name's Dowling."

THE ELUSIVE MISS DE GRUCHY

"Dowling? No, that name means nothing to me."

"Do you remember when we met at The Goring in London? When we left the hotel that day, there were two men who appeared to be old friends who had just bumped into each other. They were just outside the entrance."

Polly Armscott looked blankly at Smy. "Two men? No, I don't remember two men."

"Well, the man that followed you that day was the third man in the Hotel room. He was also in the habit of following you home."

Armscott looked appalled. "Home? He followed me home as well? This is all too much…too much for me to take in."

"Perhaps we should go back to your room. It's very cold just sitting here."

Smy and Armscott walked back to the Old Ship Hotel. As soon as they'd stepped into the entrance, Armscott began to tremble and became unsteady on her feet. Smy caught her and directed her towards a nearby chair. "Are you alright? This has all been a terrible shock for you. Shall I get you some water?"

"Yes…no. I think I need to lie down. I'll be fine. Thank you for everything you've done."

"Shall I come up to the room with you?"

Using the arms of her chair to lift herself, Polly Armscott looked increasingly fragile. "No, I think I need to be alone. Perhaps you could come back this evening? We could have dinner. I think I would like that. And I'm sure my thoughts will be much clearer."

Smy watched her slowly walk up the stairs, one hand gripping the handrail as she did so. Once she was out of sight, Smy caught the attention of the receptionist and asked if a Polly Armscott was staying at the hotel. The receptionist shook her head but checked the register all the same. "Armscott, you say? No, there's no Armscott here as far as I can see."

"Do you have a Miss de Gruchy staying here? She was the lady I was talking to over at that table just now."

Again the receptionist scanned the register. Once more, she shook her head. "I'm afraid not. Are you sure you have the right hotel?"

But Smy didn't answer and quickly walked up the stairs. As she reached the first floor, she peered down the long corridor of room doors. She repeated the same interrogation of the next two floors but decided that Armscott could have used any of the several exits from the hotel. As she reached the entrance again, the receptionist called her. "Your friend. The one you were talking to earlier. I take it that's who you were looking for? She left about three or four minutes ago."

When Smy found herself back on the coast road, she looked in vain for Armscott. Two women had now slipped from her grasp, both vital to her determination to unravel exactly what was going on. Resigned to the fact that Armscott had successfully escaped, she walked over to the other side of the coast road and spent some minutes watching the sea, desperately trying to think of what to do next.

At first she told herself that her journey to Brighton had been a wasted one but then, on reflection, realised that this was too damning a conclusion. After all, she had spotted both Armscott and Dowling making their way to Brighton on the train, and had inadvertently bumped into a figure that she knew was a link with the Framlingham murder of Ventnor.

As she walked slowly back in the direction of the guest house it occurred to her that it might be thoughtful, on her journey back to Suffolk, to call in once more to see Eleanor to offer her condolences. Although this seemed a reasonable course of action at first, a counter-argument arose in her mind that a letter offering her condolences might be more appropriate, especially given that there had been no love lost between Eleanor and Lawrence Wright. And Smy was also unsure whether it might be wise, in her heightened emotional state, to see her again so soon.

On one of the benches that she passed sat a wounded Indian soldier in a wheelchair, with an army companion standing behind him. Both men stared out across the swell of the ocean, perhaps longing for the warmth of their own country and the smiles of those they had said goodbye to. As she passed them, she noticed that the soldier in the wheelchair had an empty sleeve folded across his chest and tucked into his greatcoat. If that man should return, thought Smy, what will life now have in store for him? If he has a loved one waiting for him, how might she feel when she sees a reduced man, physically and mentally, step down off the train?

Smy exchanged a brief exchange with the two soldiers about how cold the weather was and walked on. What was she to do now? Was there anything in Brighton to stay for? Dowling, Wright and Carver, the very people who might explain what lay behind all these awful developments were now dead. Perhaps she had relied on others too much? Rather than seeking explanations, she could have focused on analysing the details of the murders to see if there was a pattern that she should have found earlier. She still shot a glance occasionally to see if, by some fortunate coincidence, she might espy the elusive Miss Armscott, but she had slipped back into the shadows. The wind was colder now and seemed to be driving even the hardiest souls indoors.

Upon reaching the house she opened the door to Mrs Walters who, with cloth in hand, was cleaning the handrail of the stairs. "Ah, Miss Smy. I'm glad I caught you. Albert brought back a telegram for you. Now, you stay there while I fetch it."

While Mrs Walters was in the small adjacent room that she called her office, Smy called in, "How has business been for you? The war must be having some effect, I presume."

Mrs Walters returned with an envelope. "Oh, I can't complain. Still got some of the usual customers and one or two new ones. I never used to get military men at one time. But, with being on the coast and everything, we have more passing through. Newhaven is so busy these days with sending everything to the front that there's sometimes not a room to be had. There's your telegram now."

"Thank you. Yes, there was a man I noticed. Very quiet at breakfast. I did wonder if he was an army man. Very reserved."

"I take it you mean Captain Joyce. Very courteous but likes to keep himself to himself, unlike Mr Todd, whom you've no doubt had the pleasure of having to listen to this morning."

"Ah, that was Mr Todd, was it? The salesman? Yes, we had words, I'm afraid."

"Yes, I heard and good for you. He's as good as gold with paying, I will give him that. That said, I'm afraid in my line you can't always be too choosy."

As soon as she closed the door of her bedroom behind her, Smy took out the telegram. It was a short reply from Manners: THINK I'VE WOMAN'S IDENTITY STOP DANGEROUS STOP

A knock on the door broke Smy's train of thought. "Who is it?"

"It's me again, Miss Smy. I'd made some tea and thought you might like a cup."

"Just one moment." Smy opened the door and Mrs Walters put the cup and saucer on a side table. "Thank you. That's really kind of you."

"And before I forget, you're obviously a woman much in demand. After you'd gone upstairs I found this envelope with your name on it. Someone must have pushed it through the letterbox. Here you are. I'll be off now and leave you in peace."

Smy took the envelope and, as had always been her habit, looked at the handwriting. It wasn't a hand that she recognised. She then realised that she'd forgotten to tell Mrs Walters that she would be leaving to return to Suffolk, and decided to do so after drinking her tea. She loosened her blouse a little and sat on the bed, took out the letter and threw the envelope to one side.

Miss Smy

I believe I have your purse which you must have dropped at lunchtime in Brighton today. As I was working, I was unable to return it but noticed the card of the hotel you are staying in, which is why I thought I would send a message. I will be at the West Pier

at 9.00 pm if you would like to meet so that I can return it to you.
  Yours sincerely
  Constance Drewer

Smy immediately snatched up her handbag and found that her purse was indeed missing. Was the message genuine? Was it Polly Armscott playing another of her manipulative games? Or was it a carefully planned hoax that she might regret falling for?

A WALK IN THE DARK

A blast of wind showered Smy's face with tiny pinpricks of icy rain. She turned her head to one side away from the sea so the brim of her hat, which she was holding down with one hand, would take the worst of each gust of rain. On the horizon, the oily smudges of clouds had now almost completely hidden the pale band of lemon that sat on the rim of the water. The walk from the guest house in York Road to the pier was only a few minutes, but the inclement weather made the journey feel so much longer.

As she drew closer to the pier, it was difficult to see anyone there at all. Smy's watch confirmed that it was almost nine o'clock and she guessed that she might be first to arrive. On each flank of the pier stood two large and identical oriental-style buildings and, as Smy peered down the length of the pier, she could just make out girders and other building materials where a new theatre was being constructed.

"Don't turn around. If you do, I will shoot you." It was a man's voice, one that she was certain she recognised. Smy estimated that he must only be a few yards behind her and remained completely still.

"Just who are you?" the man asked.

"You must already know who I am or you wouldn't have

asked me to meet you. Besides, your letter addressed me by name even though there would have been nothing in my lost purse to tell you who I was."

"Don't get clever with me. I could kill you now and have done with you. To be honest, that seems to be the best option anyway."

Looking ahead, Smy could see that no one was walking in her direction. Even the traffic - horse-drawn or motor - seemed to have hunkered down for the night and the streets were eerily empty. Far ahead she could just make out a motorcycle that was soon lost as the dark and rain slowly draped around it. "I don't think shooting an innocent person is going to help your situation. In fact, it will only give the police one more clue to…"

"Shut up! Now this is what you are going to do. You will carry on walking in the direction you are now facing. You will act like it's an ordinary evening stroll. I will be behind you and if I think you are about to try anything suspicious then I will not hesitate to kill you. Are we clear about that?"

"Quite clear. Do I call you Constance or Miss Drewer?"

"Just keep walking. You obviously inherited your comedic skills from the sadly deceased Laurie Morrie."

"Such comedic skills as I might have are my own. Where are we going?"

"A little closer to the shore. Somewhere where the sound of a bullet ripping through your skull won't be heard. Now tell me your real name and what you are doing here."

"My name is Polly Armscott."

"Don't play stupid games."

"Ah, so you know Miss Armscott?"

"I'm warning you. Killing is something I'm quite used to.

And I'm giving you a choice. You can die quickly or slowly. Either way suits me. The effort on my part is identical for either alternative."

Yes, there was something definitely familiar about the voice. Smy tried to push her worry away so that she could think. Just whose voice was it? In those precious seconds she forced herself to recall where she had heard it…

And then a single shot rang out above the wind and sea causing Smy to lurch forward with the shock of the sound. There was no pain. She was certain of that. But perhaps those who are shot do not feel any pain at first? She found that she was still gripping the brim of her hat as she stood quite still. Did one die before the pain of being shot could be felt? Behind her came the sound of someone groaning, and then she heard something metallic skittering across the pavement.

Wheeling round she could see a man hunched on the ground, his body contracting momentarily before resting. His eyes were still open as if staring intently at the sea. Smy brought up her free hand to her chest, trying to process the horror of her situation. On the pavement lay the body of Mr Joyce, the quiet man she and Mrs Walters had been talking about only that evening.

"Close one, eh?" The voice came from a man now inspecting the chambers of his pistol. As he looked up, Smy's eyes widened with surprise.

"Mr Todd!"

Todd smiled at Smy before returning his revolver to an inside pocket of his greatcoat. "Hate having to do that. Not really British in my view, shooting a man in the back. But, needs must." He quickly looked about him and motioned with his arm. "We'd best leave him to the authorities. Take my arm now and let's look like we're a normal couple."

It seemed almost surreal to Miss Smy, to slip her arm through Todd's and then casually walk away from a man whose life had ended so violently on a Brighton pavement. At first she couldn't bring herself to speak, so wrapped up as she was trying to make sense of the events of the last half hour. Of course, she told herself, it was the shock of what she had just witnessed that was making her thoughts difficult to navigate. Yet there was another factor that had undoubtedly confused her all the more: that her saviour should have been the odious Mr Todd.

"You all right, old girl?"

Smy just nodded and kept her eyes fixed towards the pavement.

"Fancy a drink? I know I could do with a pint."

"Not really. But if you want to have a drink, then I don't mind."

"Let me buy you a brandy. Just the ticket for shock, you know."

Todd seemed very un-Todd like. When he returned from the bar and placed the drinks on the table, there was something very different about him. If he hadn't been wearing the same suit and gaudy tie that he had come down to breakfast in on that morning, Smy might have thought him another man entirely.

"Is your name really Todd?"

"No. And the suit's not mine either. Or this awful bloody hat and tie. But they do their job, if you know what I mean?"

"Thank you. Thank you for what you did this evening. If you hadn't been there it would have been me they'd be taking to the mortuary."

"Not the most pleasant of men, Captain Joyce. Obviously beginning to feel a bit jittery. Would have preferred not to have done that. There'll be some explaining to do with the army. Nice gun, he had. New Webley. Shame to leave it on the pavement back there."

"Mark VI?"

He took a long draught of his beer with eyes concentrated on Smy. "Now, how come a nice woman like yourself would know something like that?"

"And why would someone posing as a travelling salesman be following a woman out on her evening walk?"

"Lucky for you I did."

"How did you know Joyce was planning to meet me?"

"I didn't at first. I spotted him in the dining room at the bureau in the corner, scribbling a note. Thought it suspicious so wanted to see what he was up to. And, sitting a little later perusing my Daily Express in the lounge, what do I see but our Captain Joyce walking out the front door and then popping a little envelope through the letterbox. Had a quick shufti and saw your name on it."

"And thought you'd better follow me?"

"Not quite. Thought I'd best follow him. And quite the ducker and diver he was as well. But careless. Inexperienced, I'd say. Here, are you going to drink that brandy or what?"

"I can't. I think the shock is beginning to wear off on its own. So what's your name? I don't know anything about you, except that you are definitely not a travelling salesman."

"Todd. Just call me Mr Todd for now. Keeps things nice and simple."

Smy took her coat off the back of her chair and stood up. "Todd it remains then. I think I'd better be going back."

"Me too. When we get there, you go in first. I'll slip into a pub and wait a while. Wouldn't want the good Mrs Walters jumping to the wrong conclusions."

As Smy and her saviour neared the junction of Western Street and Cross Street, he stopped and suggested, "You go on now. I'll see you at breakfast. I promise to be as offensive as ever."

"Of course. Can I ask you just one question? Did you know a man called Dowling?"

A half smile fell across his face and he thought carefully before he answered. "We have a lot to talk about tomorrow, Miss Smy."

"Tomorrow? When, tomorrow?"

"On the train back to London. I think it's time you met an old friend of yours. A very old friend."

A VERY OLD FRIEND

How different Brighton Station looked when bathed in the brittle morning sunlight that streamed through the glass panels of the ornate roof. Even the people who were walking across the concourse seemed to do so with a lighter step, as if spring had infused their bodies with a different, more positive urgency. Porters exchanged grins, asides and winks; the ladies behind the counter in the tea room laughed a little more readily, and even sliced more generous helpings of cake for their customers. A Lhasa Apso dog stared faithfully at her mistress, its curled question mark of a tail twitching with the pleasure of being at her side.

Walking across the station concourse came Miss Winifred Smy, carefully surveying the crowd for 'Mr Todd' who had promised to be waiting under the departure board at 10.00 am precisely. She was a little concerned as he hadn't appeared for breakfast but, true to his word, there he stood. He waved at Miss Smy who, for a moment, was taken aback as there was no sign of the apparel he'd been wearing the night before.

"You look very different."

"Oh, this?" He looked down at his suit and flicked his tie from inside his double-breasted jacket. "The acting's over for a while. I'm glad I got here on time though. The police kept me rather longer than I anticipated."

"The police?"

Todd gave a mischievous wink. "Well, let's say that we had a little story to cobble together. Apparently, some poor man was shot on the coast road last night. All very mysterious."

"Was his name Captain Joyce, by any chance?"

"Do you know, I do believe it was. Now where's our train?"

The journey back to London was uneventful, for which Miss Smy was grateful. Turning over the events of the previous evening she came to realise that the entire day had been fraught, but nothing had prepared her for the terror she felt when threatened by Joyce. As they had been joined in their compartment by a large, hamster-eyed man whose skin seemed to permanently glisten with perspiration, Todd and Smy agreed to postpone their discussions until they reached London.

Victoria Station was unusually busy. "Fancy a walk?" asked Todd.

"Where to?"

"The East India Club. About 30 minutes or so, at a reasonable pace."

"Are you under the illusion that I will be admitted into a men's club?"

"Not for a moment. But you'll see why when we get there."

They walked through Green Park and soon found themselves amongst the grand architecture of St. James Square. Reaching the entrance of the East India Club, Todd made his apologies to Miss Smy and went inside. After a few minutes, he was back with her. "First objective accomplished. Second objective over there." He nodded towards a modest building only a few yards away, tucked into the corner of the square.

Three sharp raps on the knocker was soon followed by the door being opened by a slightly bowed elderly man.

"Good afternoon, Sir."

"Afternoon, Williams. I have brought this lady with me to attend a meeting. We will soon be joined by another person."

"Very good, Sir." Williams stepped back and allowed them into the entrance hall. Despite Smy's first impression of the building, the interior revealed just how deceptive the frontage was. An overwhelming smell of wood polish hung in the air and Smy's feet were soon walking on deep pile carpets, passing through long corridors hung with fine art. They were shown into a room that had a long walnut table surrounded by high-backed chairs. Tea was ordered.

They had both just sat down when the door was opened and in burst a smartly dressed man whose tall, wiry body belied a reservoir of great energy.

"Winifred! Miss Winifred Smy! Good god. How long has it been? Twenty years? By Jove, I bet it's not far short of that number."

Smy rose and grasped the man's extended hand. "Probably that. I had no idea that…"

"That it was your old employer on your back? 'Fraid so, m' dear. Now sit down. Where's that tea, Hoskins? You have ordered some?"

"I have indeed, Sir. Miss Smy, I take it that you already know…"

"Sir Butley-Low? Yes, we were once well acquainted." She then turned to her Brighton companion. "And you are not Mr Todd, after all, Mr Hoskins?"

Sir Butley-Low cut in. "Tirpitz, if I'm not mistaken. Jolly good show that. But that was just the start of your illustrious career with us. Sorry to have lost you, Ma'am. Door always open. You know that?"

"I think my days in your service are numbered, Sir."

Butley-Low scowled. "As were those of the Secret Service Bureau that you once knew, my dear lady. All changed in 1909. Grown a lot from what you might remember. My brief is very limited now. But we've some good chaps. Sorry to have lost Dowling though. Fine man. But tell me, Hoskins, whatever was he thinking? To have wound up in such a vulnerable position. Always impetuous, Dowling. Never could quite rein him in, eh, Hoskins?"

"Quite, Sir." Hoskins agreed.

A tentative knock on the door heralded the arrival of tea and whilst it was being poured, Butley-Low began. "Now let me tell you, Miss Smy, there is no one else I'd leave a good lunch in the club for. But once I got the message that Hoskins was with you and that we should meet, well, I dropped my soup spoon immediately. Now, let's get to business! Tell us what you know, and then we'll clamber into the jolly old confessional box after you."

Smy thought it utterly incongruous to be relating, over a cup of excellent tea, the murderous deeds that took place in a small town in Suffolk to the head of an arm of the British intelligence services. Nevertheless, she informed Butley-Low and Hoskins (who, like Dowling, didn't appear to have a first name) of the murders of Ventnor and Spurling, and the sudden disappearance from the scene of Lawrence Wright and Alfred Carver. Smy also told how the murder had been contrived so as to pin the guilt on herself. Upon revealing that neither Wright or Carver had made reservations for the second evening at their hotel - even though they were due to perform for a second concert the following day - she saw the briefest exchange of eye contact pass between her two interlocutors.

Butley-Low placed down the biscuit he'd been methodically nibbling and asked, "What about the visit to the Goring with… who was it, Hoskins?"

"That would be Miss Marguerite De Gruchy, Sir, although we know it was Miss Polly Armscott all along."

"Is she an actress or something?"

"Some years before, she was, Sir. Quite the Sarah Bernhardt it appears."

"Sorry, m' dear. Do carry on."

Smy then picked up the narrative once more: her lunch with Miss De Gruchy; the return to London for a meeting with Polly Armscott that eventually revealed that she and Miss de Gruchy were one and the same person; Smy's meeting with Dowling and the subsequent flight to Brighton on Eleanor Wright's suggestion that her brother, Lawrence, might be found there.

"And that's where you ran into our man, Hammond."

"Hammond? I'm sorry, Sir Butley-Low. I don't recall a Mr Hammond."

"Station porter. Would have told you to choose Mrs Walters' fine establishment."

"He was one of your men?"

Hoskins stood up when he heard a knock at the door and a woman, whom Smy assumed to be one of the secretaries, entered. "The file you asked for, Mr Hoskins."

"Thank you, Mrs Hallam. If I might answer your question, Miss Smy, he was one of ours indeed. As soon as we had the word that you were making your way to Brighton on the same train as Armscott and Dowling, we needed to make sure that you didn't 'queer the pitch', if you catch my meaning."

"And the next day, m' dear, you walked into a hotel room and found three dead men: Messrs Lawrence and Carver, and our man Dowling."

"Unfortunately, I did."

"Hoskins, can our budget stretch to a more exciting biscuit? These are drearier than a London smog. Sorry, m' dear, I interrupted you. Dashed uncivil. Tell me what you noticed."

"That it was a set-up to look like they had fallen out over the cards. I think that Dowling had somehow made the acquaintance of Lawrence Wright and Alfred Carver, probably by convincing Wright that he also had a fondness for gambling. The killer had watched the three men return to Wright's hotel room and then found some way to wheedle their way in. Carver's body had been dragged to the doorway of the bathroom. That was obvious from the smears of blood on the carpet. I'm not sure why he was dragged there. Perhaps to make it look as if there had been a confused exchange of gunshots. Whoever did it knew that Lawrence, if he wasn't betting on the horses, always fell back on his second obsession which was stud poker."

Butley-Low dunked his biscuit whilst keeping his eyes fixed on Smy. "Poker, eh? Made it look like there'd been an argument and out came the ironmongery. Was that what we were supposed to believe?"

"That's what the Brighton constabulary believes. But the way the cards had been arranged was all wrong. They were all face down, so how could they have known that the other party was cheating, as they hadn't yet shown their cards? And, as I pointed out at the time, stud poker only has one card face down. Definitely not five."

"You seem to know an awful lot about the pleasures of

betting. Has one become a cardsharp since we last met?"

"Lawrence's sister and I became firm friends when I first came to London. At parties and the like, one couldn't avoid witnessing the peccadilloes of her brother."

Butley-Low stood up and poured himself more tea. "Miss Smy?"

"I haven't finished this one yet, thank you."

He took his cup and saucer and walked over to the window. "Fine day. Yes, a fine day. Anything else strike you as… unusual?"

"The gun. The revolver on the table. It was a Webley Mark VI. Exactly the same type of gun that was planted in my pocket after the first Framlingham murder. It was also the same gun that Captain Joyce had last night. For a gun that has been assigned exclusively for military use, there do seem to be a lot of them about."

Butley-Low nodded and sipped a little of his tea. "This woman who tried to make it look as if you did the murder. You said that you were certain that you ran into her again just before you found the three bodies in the hotel room. How do you know?"

"Because there exists a type of person who believes that failing to attend to the most basic sanitary procedures can be successfully masked by the application of cheap perfume. Unfortunately, sweat soon combines with unwashed linen and creates the most unappealing scent. As soon as I smelled her outside the hotel, I knew her to be the same woman. Do you know who she is?"

Hoskins held up the file that had just been brought into the room. "We most certainly do."

ELEPHANTS AND LYONS

"Ah, Lydia Lyons," confirmed Nigel Manners. He and Smy were ambling through the churchyard of St. Michael's, a stone's throw from Framlingham Castle.

"And she was the one that you warned me about in your telegram. However did you find out about her? You seem to know almost as much as my London contacts."

Manners crossed his thin arms in what appeared to Miss Smy to be a rather uncomfortable position. "It was not so difficult. But tell me first, who were these London contacts of yours? You intrigue me. Police? Or perhaps some nefarious Government agency."

Smy had noticed a thread working itself loose from the button of her cuff and began to carefully wind it around her forefinger. "No need to pry, Mr Manners. I am such a dull person. How could I possibly know anyone remotely interesting in London?"

"You're a wily one. You know and I know that your life was and is anything but dull. Wasn't it I that confronted you about your disruptive activities when we first met? Those things you got up to when you were in your salad days. Green in judgment and cold in blood." Manners provokingly started to hum the melody of Ethel Smyth's *'The March of the Women'*.

"You still haven't answered my question about Lydia Lyons."

"Oh, I didn't have to look very far. Asked around really. Had anyone noticed anyone strange around the time of the concert? It was old Rollins, the station master who gave me the first clue. He told me that when the train from Ipswich arrived and everyone got out, there was someone shouting from one of the carriages that her purse had been stolen. Such a hue and cry went up from this poor woman that all the passengers who had just got off the train turned to see what all the fuss was about."

"Except for one passenger?"

"You never cease to amaze me. That's right, except for one passenger who just kept calmly walking to the station exit. Little woman, he said."

Smy yanked at the thread and cleanly snapped it from her cuff. "And then?"

"And then Rollins told the police. They found her drifting around the market square and brought her in for questioning."

"And the purse?" The irony of what had been stolen was not lost on Smy.

"Long gone. She denied all knowledge of the event. Cool as a cucumber, the police said. But she did have, on her person, a note addressed to her which began with 'Dear Lydia...'"

"Damn, now I've lost the button!" Smy looked behind her to see where it might have fallen. "Carry on. Did it give only her first name?"

"It did. They asked if she was staying in Framlingham that evening and where. And she told them."

Smy found the errant button and placed it inside her skirt pocket. "And where did she tell them she'd be staying?"

"Samuel Spurling's house, no less. Rather curious, don't you think? Not really Spurling's type, I'd say."

Smy looked sharply at Manners, trying to see where this information might be leading. "Did she give her full name to the officers?"

"She was very reluctant to do so. But our Mr Spurling was more forthcoming, especially when faced with the good men of our local constabulary. As the police had proof that he had written to her, they were insistent that he communicate the dear Lydia's address. Once I had the name and address..."

"How did you get the name and address from the police?"

"Oh, Miss Smy. Surely you above all people appreciate that a trade such as mine depends on the close relationships we enjoy with our fellow professionals. Besides, the officer concerned was, shall we say, in my debt and glad to return a small favour I once granted him."

"A favour? You have to tell me."

"Well, but we must keep this to ourselves, I had two tickets to some dreadful opera which my editor insisted I write a review of. The constable concerned had started to frequent the company of a young woman in Colchester who had communicated a desire to see said opera but, to the constable's dismay, all tickets had sold out."

"So you reluctantly donated your own."

"Well, I couldn't think of a worse evening than watching some tenants of a dreary Parisian garret bemoaning their sordid lives in song. What pleasure others see in such a spectacle is utterly beyond my comprehension."

"What about the review?"

"Oh, once I had the programme I called an old friend of mine given to such dubious enjoyments and he kindly dictated the bones of the piece to me. Editor loved it and everyone was happy."

Smy's face suddenly bore a puzzled look and she tried to ask, as neutrally as she could, "This policeman, was it Inspector Tranmer?"

"Ah, you think it was dear Miss Clemence who was the opera-loving woman in question? Well, it wasn't and, besides, she doesn't live in Colchester and our good Mr Tranmer is not a constable. Now do tell me, why do you want to know?"

Smy stopped and looked up at the sky. "Rain, Mr Manners? Anyway, let's get back to the matter at hand."

Manners' shrewd face revealed that the supposed disinterested manner of Smy's inquiry had not been successful. "Ok, let's return to Miss Lydia Lyons. She's a south London girl. A person given to hoisting."

"A pickpocket?"

Manners, clearly enjoying being able to communicate the fruits of his research, curved his thumbs inside the lapels of his jacket. "A pickpocket, a burglar, a woman given to loitering in large department stores in the company of her female colleagues."

"Doing what?"

"Stealing. Not just small items, but whipping items of great value beneath their skirts to pass on to the McDonalds' Elephant and Castle mob, who then fence the goods and reward the dear ladies handsomely for their troubles."

"I take it that this came from one of your London contacts?"

"Indeed it did. Dear Dickie Weedon. Contacts everywhere, that man. He's been tracking both the Elephant and Castle mob as well as the Forty Elephants gang. It is the latter which our Lydia Lyons is a member of."

"*Was* a member of, I think you'll find."

Manners raised his eyebrows in surprise. "I think that you are more up-to-date about Miss Lyons than I. These London people you know are jolly good. Any chance that you might introduce me to them?"

Winifred Smy leaned her back against one side of the church porch. "You were right about how dangerous Lydia Lyons is and I am very grateful that you sent me that telegram. I am going to be open with you, Mr Manners. Although what I do have to tell you will be only part of what I know. The rest will have to wait and, to be frank, I may never divulge it to you, or to anyone."

Smy had never seen Manners so calm before. His usual gangly demeanour had been stilled as if frozen by some Grimm's fairy-tale witchery. A twitch of his right eye was the only sign that revealed his complete enthralment with Smy's secret. "But you know I will find out, Miss Smy? The rest of what you know, I mean. It's my calling. And such a calling is one to which I must always comply."

'We'll see. Now, do you want me to tell you or shall I leave you to find out in your own way?"

Manners, his innate awkwardness returning once more, guffawed as he turned in a complete circle before momentarily losing his balance. "Oh, the floor is entirely yours! Look at me, am I not all ears?"

"As you say, Lydia Lyons was part of the Forty Elephants gang. But she had one rather troubling weakness, one that I had witnessed for myself on two occasions. You are right when you say that their *modus operandi* was to visit the more fashionable London stores dressed as women of a more elevated class. At the time, their leader was Diamond Alice. She was the one who threw Lyons out. She realised that her body odour was getting noticed and was not what one might expect of a more refined woman in a smart department store."

"Ah, so that is why she's turning up instead in seaside towns, dipping her nimble fingers into the pockets and bags of the unsuspecting holiday makers. And very good at it she is too, I understand."

Smy looked up and down the length of the path that ran through the churchyard, making sure that no one was near before continuing. "And it was in Brighton that Spurling first spotted her."

"Spurling? What was he doing in Brighton?"

"That, I can't tell you. But what I can tell you is that they were often seen together. The theory is that he saw her 'hoisting' and threatened her that he would go to the police unless she did something for him."

Manners seemed to become suddenly appalled. "What do you mean 'something'? Do you mean…you know…something carnal?"

Smy laughed and shook her head. "You are a prude some-times, Manners. Well, it was something rather worse than carnal."

"You mean…"

"That's right. He wanted her to kill someone."

A PERFUMED SCARF

"Miss Smy, isn't it?"

"That's correct. I am here to see Inspector Tranmer. He asked to see me."

The Police Sergeant put down his pen and promised that he wouldn't be long, before disappearing into a back office. Smy listened intently to hear any snatches of conversation that might give away why Tranmer had wanted to see her, but the conversation was too muffled even for her excellent hearing.

The sergeant came out again and asked her to follow him. She was expecting to be taken into one of the interview rooms but found herself shown instead into a small office. Behind the desk stood Tranmer, obviously pleased to welcome her in.

"I apologise for the room. A bit pokey, really. But it's private and, after your last visit here, I didn't think you'd want to be reacquainted with any of our other rooms."

Winifred Smy sat down on the chair immediately opposite Tranmer. "Well, I appreciate your thoughtfulness. My history with this police station is, shall we say, somewhat chequered."

As Tranmer eased himself into his own chair, its old leather creaked like a rusted hinge. "Now Miss Smy, after the rather misguided way we communicated with you after the murder in the Assembly Hall, I felt the least I could do was to give you an update on something new which has come to my attention."

Smy removed her gloves. "How's Miss Clemence? In good health, I hope?"

"Maud? Oh yes, she's…she's good."

"You don't seem very sure. I do hope that all is well between you both?"

Tranmer sucked in his cheeks a little, and then briskly suggested, "Let's return to the matter in hand, shall we?"

"Of course, but tell me first, do you like this scent?" Smy offered her scarf to Tranmer who, a little bemused, gave the garment a cursory sniff. "Yes. Very nice. Very…very you."

"But not Maud. She wouldn't like it, I suppose?"

A frustrated sigh from Tranmer told Smy that he was becoming increasingly annoyed. "The matter in hand, I think. Horace Ventnor."

Smy's playful attitude ceased immediately and she not only sat erect but slightly leaned forward towards Tranmer. "Ventnor? Forgive me. Do please continue."

"Thank you. As you'll recall, the appearance of Ventnor was confusing to many. No one seemed to know him and yet he obviously had access to Laurie Morrie's dressing room. So we can perhaps take from that that they must have been acquainted. We had enquiries made in London and found out some surprising facts. First, he was a man of some means. An accountant, no less. And a well-respected one at that."

"But, as we both recently agreed, a man with a certain weakness for a particular actress."

"Yes, he was by all accounts completely obsessed."

"I have been drawing many thoughts together from, if I may be permitted to use the phrase, my own enquiries. Would the actress in question be a Miss Polly Armscott?"

Tranmer opened a brown manila folder on his desk and scanned a sheet inside. "Indeed, Miss Polly Armscott. Although to call her an actress is being a tad incorrect. She's not been on the stage for several years, she's now apparently…"

"Working in Admiralty House?"

Tranmer threw an inquisitive glance at Smy. "Have I brought you here under false pretences? You seem to already know a lot of what I was going to share with you."

"I do appreciate you asking me here, Inspector. It gives me a chance to clarify my own thoughts and suspicions. I believe that Ventnor was enticed here by Lawrence Wright - or Laurie Morrie if you prefer - for one thing: to take Wright's place in his dressing room. How did he entice Ventnor into taking his place, probably by convincing him that the next person who would be joining him in the dressing room would be Polly Armscott. So why would he want Ventnor to assume his place? Because Wright must have known beforehand that his life was in danger. By getting Ventnor to assume his identity and to take his place in the dressing room, and then disappearing immediately he left the stage, he thought he would be able to fool the killer."

"Wright appears to be a man who had no qualms about sacrificing others to save his own skin. Yes, as far-fetched as it sounds, it does seem to square up with the reservations at The Crown Hotel."

"Exactly. I also checked that with Mr Sewell, the manager. Why would Wright and Carver only book one night when they were appearing in two performances over two evenings? We both know exactly why: because they knew what was about to happen. They had absolutely no intention of staying for a second night."

Tranmer leaned back in his chair, accompanied by one more leathery squeak, and tapped his fingers on the folder on his desk. "So who would want him dead? And who tipped him off that his life was in danger?"

"Not only tipped him off, but must have conveyed the exact time and manner of the attack."

"Poor Ventnor. A rather grisly end to a misplaced passion."

"Poor Ventnor, indeed. He was a hapless victim who was involved in something utterly beyond his understanding."

"I hear you've been away for a couple of days. Brighton, I understand."

Smy bristled a little with the manner of Tranmer's observation. "I understand that, even in a time of war, one still has the right to a private life."

Herbert Tranmer picked up the file that lay under his hand and put it in the middle of three stacked trays on his desk. "Winifred, let's not play games here. I brought you in perhaps against my better judgment. Superintendent Freeman has told us that this case is no longer a priority. He offered no explanation. He wasn't disposed to explain why. Two murders in our patch and it is, apparently, no longer a priority."

Smy said nothing, but her look conveyed a sympathy for Tranmer's strange predicament. Somehow, she felt that the world was out of kilter with Tranmer, that the events of the last few weeks had removed all that was familiar: the purpose of his calling, and the ambiguity of this maddening woman that would not release her hold on him.

"Have you spoken to Nigel Manners, Herbert?" The mention of his first name in that moment seemed to brighten his spirits.

"Had him in this morning. Especially when I heard about the source of Duckworth's opera tickets."

"So you know all about Lydia Lyons and Spurling?"

"As I'm sure you do, too. You see, Miss Smy, I am at this moment sitting at a small desk in a small town in a county that doesn't even have a city. A music hall star comes to my small town and causes the violent death of an innocent man. This music hall star then disappears. All too soon, a second death follows that of the first, when a citizen of the same town is found stabbed in his own home. A man that has a strange relationship with a well-known thief and burglar all the way from South London."

Smy's face softened as she watched Tranmer relax into his story.

"First, Sibley makes a right dog's breakfast of the investigation. And then I find that he is pulled away from the case and the murders of two people are not as important as a little old lady's lost cat, or someone in Brabling Green stealing a bag of tea. So I thought to myself, 'there is something much more to this than meets the eye' and set off to humble Kenton to invoke the assistance of a certain Miss Smy. But she's not there. The neighbours were of no help. So I accept that you are absent and then who do I run into at the post office, but a Mr Nigel Manners, receiving a telegram from your good self."

"And he told you I was in Brighton."

"He was very helpful. And then what do I find? That the grim reaper had eventually caught up with Messrs Wright and Carver and some other unfortunate at a card game that had spiralled out of control. Rather a coincidence, Miss Smy."

A sharp knock on the door interrupted their conversation. It was the police sergeant from the front desk. "Sorry to interrupt you, Sir, but a Miss Clemence is out front. Said she would like a word."

"Maud?"

"Yes, Sir."

The sergeant abruptly left with an instruction that Tranmer would be out soon. Smy could see that Maud's visit was an unexpected one. "I think I might be in the way, Inspector."

"No, no. Wait a moment. I think we need to continue this conversation. Maybe not now, but very soon."

Smy gathered her things and stood up. "Will you be showing her into this room, Inspector?"

"I don't know. It all depends how long she needs to talk and whatever it is she wants to talk about."

"Then you might want to open that small window. This perfume might be very discreet, but it does tend to linger for a good while."

Smy walked breezily out into the reception area of the station. Maud wheeled around expecting to see Tranmer before her rather than Smy, her face being a mixture of surprise and barely concealed indignation.

"Hello, Miss Clemence. How lovely to see you. We've finished now. I'm sure Herbert will be out to see you presently. Oh, thank you very much, Sergeant. A good day to you both."

A WARNING FOR POLLY

How strange it felt for Miss Smy to walk out of Walham Green Station again and take in the long view down the Fulham Road. It seemed almost impossible to think that it was at this very place on the concourse that Dowling had confronted her, but now he too was dead. A shiver ran through her as she contemplated that the killing may not be over, and that Smy herself might be on the growing list of victims before this mystery was fully resolved.

She now found herself at the intersection of two authorities: the East Suffolk Constabulary and the Secret Service Bureau. The former had become, over the last few years, increasingly known to her. As for the SSB, it had once been significant to her when she was, in an admittedly long-distant way, involved in its dealings. She smiled inwardly as she recalled Dowling's summation of her Tirpitz adventure, as if she had been some silent movie star collared by a devoted fan on the London streets.

It had been a pleasant enough day. Once more she had lingered outside the Admiralty Building as the various workers had left for their respective homes, but there was no Polly Armscott. She didn't think that there would be, but it had given her more hope that the second part of her search might be fruitful. Once more, she was soon walking along Dawes Road to the house that she had once seen Armscott disappear into on that first evening.

She stepped up to the door and knocked. As before, a ground-floor light appeared in the window to her right and then fell across the hallway. It was the same woman as before but this time, not wanting to be caught off-guard again, Smy asked jauntily, "Is Mr Carver in?"

"Who's arskin'?"

"I'm Lizzie, Alfred's sister. Perhaps 'is wife's in? She'll be quite 'appy to see me. To be honest, she sent me a letter to say she's a bit outa sorts. Asked if I'd come and see 'er. You've probably noticed she's not been herself, what wiv all those strange people asking to see 'er and everyfink."

The woman's face seemed to show that she had been taken in by Smy's confident performance. "Sister, you say?"

"Don't tell me our Alf hasn't told you? The useless big piece of string. Once he'd got in with that theatre crowd 'e didn't have any time for his family. And now he's gone off and left 'is poor wife on her own with every bloomin' Tom, Dick 'n' Harry arsking after 'er. Now, don't let me keep you standin' 'ere in the cold. Point me at the room an' I'll leave yer to yer evenin'."

The woman stopped back and pointed up the stairs. "Up there, back on yourself and it's the door facin' yer. Tell 'er I was asking after 'er."

"Too kind. Now I won't disturb yer a moment longer." Smy was glad to see the woman go back into her own room, finding that, as happened when she pretended to be Ventnor's wife in the hotel in Framlingham, the accent she was trying to simulate was beginning to sound unconvincing.

It was obvious that, although clean enough, the house had not seen any decoration for many years. There was a telltale odour that spoke of myriad residents staying for a short while before continuing their downtrodden lives elsewhere. Reaching the top of the stairs, Smy did a U-turn on the first landing and could see the door the woman had indicated. There was a flickering light which was ebbing in the thin space at the bottom of the door.

Smy tapped gently and then turned the handle. The door was unlocked and she carefully opened it. "Polly? It's me, Winifred Smy." The light in the room from the gas lamp was low and it was only by degrees that Smy could make out the hunched figure of Polly Armscott in a chair tucked into the far corner of the room.

Smy noticed a tumbler on the nearby table and a bottle of what she took to be gin, half drained of its contents. Polly Armscott looked up without any response or recognition evident on her face. Perhaps it was the sickly light of the lamp, but she appeared washed out and pale, which only accentuated the redness of her eyes.

"How did you get in here?"

"I pretended I was Alfred's sister. A cheap trick but I had to find you."

"You knew it was Alfred's room?"

Smy placed down her bag and walked over so that she could sit on the edge of the unmade bed. "It's funny how things strike you long after the event. I'd fallen for the line that you were Lawrence's girlfriend. And then two small things came back to me only recently. I was talking to Lawrence's sister and I asked her where Alfred lived these days. She said she didn't know, but that it was 'over Fulham way' or something like that. Of course, it didn't mean he necessarily lived here, but it struck me as something of a coincidence, he being an East End man and all that."

"How did you know I lived here?"

"Don't you remember me telling you that I knew you were being followed? When we met in Brighton that day. Before you disappeared again from the hotel. Every night you were being trailed by men who wanted to keep an eye on you."

Polly Armscott turned her face to the wall. "But how did you know about me and Alfred?" She spoke faintly, as if life had completely overwhelmed her.

"Again, I didn't think it at the time, but when I told you about the killing of Lawrence and Alfred, it was Alfred's death that had most affected you, not Lawrence's."

"Quite the Sherlock, aren't you?" As flat as the tones were when she spoke, Smy could still detect a degree of venom in her voice.

"Maybe, but I can't let things go. It's an obsession, I suppose. We both know that it might have been me in the dock for murder. That's what Lawrence wanted, wasn't it?"

"I don't care what Lawrence wanted. It was my Alf I cared about. But he was always under Lawrence's thumb. He never got over being stagestruck. As for Lawrence, he had Alf wrapped around his little finger."

"And Horace Ventnor? Did you have him wrapped around your little finger?"

"Silly man! I couldn't ever get rid of him. When I was in anything, he'd be there every night. In one of the front rows. Just leering at me. Then I'd have to fight him off at the stage door. Even told him about Alf and me, but he was impossible! Wouldn't leave me alone."

"And is that why you packed it in? To give yourself a quieter life?"

Polly reached for the bottle and filled the tumbler three-quarters full. "Want some?"

Smy shook her head. "Not for me."

"Yes, got the job in the… well, you know where."

Smy looked around the small bedroom, the pale green shadow of the gin bottle leaping in small jerks as the gas lamp sputtered. The wallpaper, with its washed-out smudges of red and yellow spring flowers, was beginning to peel at various places as if signalling that its long relationship with the wall would soon be over. The unmistakable smell of damp hung in the air, the scent reminding Smy of a rotting woodland log nestling in a bed of decaying autumn leaves.

"And why the whole charade with the Marguerite de Gruchy character? Was that Alfred's idea?"

There was a fleeting smile that passed over Polly's face before she answered. "No, that was Lawrence's brainwave. He'd got worried when he heard that the police released you. Wanted to know just how much you knew. So he asked me if I could find things out. Get to know you. Gain your trust."

"But why go to all the trouble you did? The stationery and grand clothes and everything."

"Because once Lawrence had convinced me to do it, I wanted to do it in my own way. It was a chance to be someone again. Not to be, not to be…well, living somewhere like this. Got the clothes from a clothes hire place in Victoria. Looked the part, didn't I?"

Winifred Smy didn't have the heart to tell her that she had seen through the disguise within minutes of them sitting down to lunch. Looking at Polly now, it was almost impossible to believe that the supremely vivacious and captivating Marguerite de Gruchy and the depressed and defeated Polly Armscott were one and the same woman.

"Did you know about what was going to happen to Ventnor? Lawrence convincing him to take his place?"

"I'm not saying. I'm not saying anything to anyone."

"All right, but tell me, how bad had Lawrence Wright's gambling habits become? He had problems when I first knew him - cards, horses, boxing - there didn't seem to be anything he wouldn't bet on. But he would always come out top in cards, however much money he lost elsewhere."

"Don't talk to me about it. It got to the stage where he was asking Alf for a loan." Polly sneered as she said this. "A loan, huh. There was never a chance of getting one penny back."

"And so he turned to other ways of getting the money?"

Polly Armscott looked up with a fierce glare. "Is that why you're here? Are you with the police? Because if you are, you'll get nothing out of me. Not you, not anyone."

Smy rose and picked up her things. "I don't think you've got anything to tell the police that they now don't already know. And a certain arm of the law has known about it for quite some time. That was why you had company every time you went to and from work."

"You're lying! You're just making it up! You are from the police, aren't you?"

"I'm going, Polly. But let me give you a warning. There is another woman, the one who killed your husband as well as Lawrence Wright. I don't know how much you know about what happened in Framlingham the night Mr Ventnor was killed, but she appears to be gunning for anyone connected with the whole affair. If I were you, I'd walk to the nearest police station and give myself up. They are soon going to come looking for you anyway."

"Then if they know about me, why haven't they locked me up already?"

"I can only guess that they still think there are other links you might have. The choice is yours. Tell them what you know and see the war out in safety. Or carry on as you are, and end up the same way as Lawrence and Alfred."

Polly Armscott took a deep slug of the gin and returned her gaze to the unprepossessing wallpaper. Smy checked she had everything and went to leave.

"What about this woman you mentioned? How will I know her?"

"That's the problem. Believe me, Polly, by the time you've realised it's her, it will be too late."

"What about you? Are you on her list?"

"If I wasn't on her list before, I'm most certainly on it now."

A VISITOR FOR SMY

The previous evening, Winifred Smy had left Polly Armscott's flat and made her way back to East London. Knowing that it was too late to get back to Kenton, she had booked a room at the Great Eastern Hotel, only a stone's throw from Liverpool Street Station. She'd looked up at the tall red brick facade and felt that it would allow her the comfort and safety she longed for that evening.

The next day, after breakfast, she'd caught the early morning train back to Ipswich and then changed for Haughley, arriving just in time to board the local train, 'The Middy', that would take her to Kenton Junction. The small engine, with its modest complement of passenger and livestock carriages, eased through the Suffolk landscape, stopping at the tiny stations that hung like small pearls strung along a silver braid.

The Station Manager, Percy Whiting, as punctilious as ever, had made a mental note of who was in the respective carriages as the train came to a halt, and opened the doors for the two passengers who were ready to alight at his station.

"Miss Smy. Been on your travels again?"

"Out and about, Mr Whiting. Oh, it's much windier here than in London."

"Always is. No big buildings to protect us 'ere. Open to the elements, we are. Now, hold yew hard there, my good woman. Seeing yew 'as made me think of summat. Now, whatever wuz it?" Percy Whiting pushed his cap back on his head and stared at the ground waiting for the memory to surface. "Of course! Thas it! A strange mawther, and no mistake. Askin' arter yew she wuz. Did I know 'er, she asked."

"Was she looking for me?"

"Right enough, she wuz. Knew yer name. Knew yew lived 'ere. Just don't know where. Then one o' the porters, ol' blabbermouth 'enry, told 'er where she'd find yew."

Smy felt a creeping fear rise inside her. "This woman. How would you describe her?"

Whiting now took his hat off completely, needing the cool air to calm his temples when so much thought was suddenly required.

"Describe 'er…'ow would I describe 'er? Well, I'm not the world's best at rememberin' a mawther I've only seen just the once, but she wuz a small thing. Not from round 'ere. Not even Essex."

"A London accent?"

"Why, I think you 'ave it there'. Talked strange. Yes, London'd dew it."

Smy knew it must be Lydia Lyons. It was too much of a coincidence. What was she to do? Avoid home even though this woman may not be there, or face her down and attempt to somehow appease her into giving herself up to the police. In her bones, she knew that the latter scenario was not an option. She had killed too much and stepping into a police station was as good as stepping into the loop of the hangman's noose.

The road from the station to her own home was less than a mile, but it felt a lonely and long trudge as if it was she that was walking to the gibbet. Would she be in the house waiting for her? She seldom locked any of the doors. Why would she? The village was small and tightly knit; most people saw everybody's comings and goings. If only she could meet someone on the way to see if they had seen the same woman Percy Whiting spoke of. Yet the Eye Road was uncommonly quiet with only the chirruping of birdsong to accompany her.

The front door was closed but she could see that the gate to the right of the house had been opened. Perhaps, thought Smy, she could surprise her. She removed her shoes and carefully placed them by the hedge next to her bag. Keeping close to the wall, she edged to the corner of the house and slowly peered around into the rear garden. Her view was limited, although a rustle of leaves - against a skirt perhaps? - caused her to jerk her head back. She tried to control her breath and remained absolutely immobile for some seconds. A footstep sounded on the stone path that ran across the back of the house. Then another. Soon a steady tread told Smy that her interloper was moving towards her. To Smy's relief, she remembered a lead doorstop that she kept behind the gate she had just come through, which she always placed there to keep the gate closed when the wind would curl around the house and rattle it endlessly, keeping her awake at night. She picked the doorstop up and held it ready to club her attacker. The sound of the footsteps grew nearer. They were still slow but she knew that she must now only be a matter of feet from her visitor. She raised the doorstop ready to strike and...

"Mr Manners!"

Manners suddenly emitted a high-pitched yell, stepped backwards and failed to see the wheelbarrow that was immediately behind him and, completely losing his balance, was flung backwards into the herbaceous border. Looking up in a state of terror he cried, "Good god, Miss Smy! What are you doing?"

"Mr Manners. I would ask you the same thing. You gave me the fright of my life! What are you skulking around my garden for?"

Manners jumped up from the border and tried to reassemble his long limbs into their previous configuration. He then patted down the leaves and petals that had been violently strewn across his suit. Smy laughed out loud, more in relief than at Manners' comedic pratfall.

Once Manners had returned to some degree of normality, a fresh confusion was evident on his face. "Your shoes, Miss Smy. Where are your shoes?" He then immediately turned away, as if Smy was the bathing Susanna and he one of the two elders forced to avert their eyes.

Smy looked down having completely forgotten that she was still without her shoes and, feeling now the cold of the flagstones rising through the soles of her feet, looked for her footwear and bag.

"Mr Manners, I apologise for what happened but…oh, let's go inside and I'll make you a pot of tea."

"And maybe a slice of cake, Miss Smy?"

"And maybe a slice of cake."

THE SCENT OF AN EXCLUSIVE

"Of course, I shouldn't be here." The words Manners spoke were just discernible through the chomping of the sponge. Once the slice had been consumed, he again reverted to his usual custom of methodically searching out every remaining crumb.

"Another slice?"

His face lit up like a child's. "Would that be OK? It's rather wonderful. I only hope that Beatrice will master producing cakes to the Smy standard."

"Well, you might want to consider baking the cakes yourself. It doesn't have to fall to Beatrice only doing the baking."

Manners was a little startled by Smy's suggestion. "What, me bake a cake? Oh, Miss Smy, if I didn't know you better I would have sworn you were being serious there for a moment."

A raised eyebrow showed that Smy could see that there was little to be gained from pursuing the argument. She put another slice of sponge on Manners' plate and topped up the tea in her own cup. "Anyway, as you were saying, why shouldn't you be here?"

"Oh, because of the business with the editor. You know, telling me not to occupy myself with these two murders. But I can't help myself. I am the irrepressible toper who will not deny himself the pleasures of the grape and grain. My instinct tells me that I must ignore his command and pursue the story."

"But secretly of course."

"Oh yes. It wouldn't do to lose my job when I am betrothed to the most beautiful woman in all the land. No, unemployment would severely impede the path that leads towards marital bliss. Anyway, since we last met, a couple of things have come my way. Thought you'd like to know."

"About Lydia Lyons?"

"Well, what with your capital contacts in London, you probably already know, but I thought I'd pass them on to you anyway. When we last met in Framlingham, you told me that the reason Lyons was thrown out of The Forty Elephants gang was because she smelled. But there was more to it than that."

Smy looked surprised. "Well, it sounds like this might be something I don't know. What was the other reason?"

"She's unstable. Very unstable. There was the mysterious case of her husband, Harold Lyons. Our lovely Lydia apparently claimed that he'd been out on a burglary and was shot by the householder. Managed to make his way back south of the river and crawled into their home and expired in their downstairs room."

"That seems credible enough to me. Why mysterious?"

Manners placed his now-empty plate back on the table. "Mysterious because there was not one drop of blood on the street, either outside the house or anywhere on the route he would have taken on his return home. All of the poor man's blood seemed to be on the floor in his own house."

Winifred Smy could feel the peril of her own situation intensifying as she listened. "What did the police do? Surely they would have reached the same conclusion?"

"I don't think the police really care. Lyons was a fully signed-up member of the Elephant and Castle Mob, and they just seemed happy enough that the gang was one man less."

"Does your contact know why she might have killed him?"

"Well, that brings me to my second point. Dickie's Forty Elephants' contact says that Lydia Lyons is a very vengeful sort. She will not let matters rest when she feels that she has been short-changed in any way. Harold Lyons always had a roving eye and yet it appeared that, even though Lydia was fully aware of his infidelity, she outwardly said and did nothing."

"So she waited patiently for the right moment to exact her revenge, if that's indeed what happened."

Manners drank what remained of his tea. "My theory is that it was Lydia who killed Samuel Spurling. Perhaps they had fallen out and, as she did for poor Harold, she made him pay the ultimate price."

"The ultimate price? Are we letting our Grub Street language run away with us, Mr Manners? No, Lydia didn't kill Samuel Spurling. I could let you continue with that delusion but would hate to think of you pursuing your prey down a blind alley."

Within a moment Manners demeanour suddenly changed. "You know, Miss Smy, the scent of an exclusive has suddenly wafted its presence and been detected by my journalistic senses. You seem very certain it wasn't Lydia Lyons that killed Spurling, so I assume you already know who the real killer is?"

Picking up the cups, saucers and plates, Winifred Smy rose and placed them by the sink. "When we were in Framlingham, I told you quite clearly that I would not divulge everything I knew. If you were to find out by independent means who Spurling's killer was, then that would be your prerogative. I will not tell you and you would be well advised to follow the advice of your editor in this matter."

"But Miss Smy, we have always been open with each other! Surely there are no secrets when it comes to the murder of a local man? I thought that we had a transparent and candid relationship. But now, I feel you don't trust me. Me, that has been so faithful to…"

"Oh, do stop your wheedling, Mr Manners. It is grating and childish. If I could tell you then I would tell you. Plain and simple. But do desist from acting like some wronged Romeo. And if you're going to sulk about it, then do so in some place other than under my roof."

Manners slumped petulantly in his chair, thrusting his bony hands deep into his trouser pockets. "Well, what does it matter? Even if you told me, the editor wouldn't run with the story anyway."

"Quite. And who knows? There may come a day when the truth about Spurling's death becomes public knowledge. So bide your time."

With his chin pressed into his chest and his lower lip jutting out, Manners looked like a scolded schoolboy. But then, as Manners typically was prone to do, he sprang from his chair and raised three fingers. "A third thing I have also found out! I nearly forgot!"

Smy laughed at Manners' sudden change of mood. "Oh, so there is a third thing. And what would that be?"

"Samuel Spurling was a fraud! He had no musical qualifications. Not a single one!"

Smy looked sympathetically at Nigel Manners but decided not to answer. She already knew that Spurling was no more a music teacher than she was, but to agree or disagree with Manners' findings would just take the conversation back to her having to defend how she could have known this. She realised that she would have liked to have relayed the full story to Manners; after all, it would probably be the crowning scoop of his career, but she couldn't allow herself to do that.

"Well, perhaps your editor might go with that story?"

Manners frowned. "No, I don't think so. I think there is something untouchable about Samuel Spurling but I can't fathom what it is. And, in all fairness, what does it matter? Why bother about the fake certificates on his wall when the poor man is now six feet under?"

"I think that's wise, Mr Manners. Now, I really must be getting on, but thank you for what you told me. It has really helped and I will repay you one day, believe me. How is Miss Bartholomew, by the way?"

"Up to her neck in matrimonial preparations. Oh, I'm very excited. I can't think what she sees in me, sometimes. I know I'm a very fine catch and everything although, to be perfectly honest, her family are a little below my station. But what does that matter? A love that effortlessly traverses the class divide! Now there's a story, if ever I had one."

'Well," Smy persisted. "As I was saying…"

"I'm going, I'm going! *Au revoir ma chère mademoiselle Smy!*"

Eventually, Smy watched the gangling form of Manners walk breezily down the Eye Road. Over the years that she had come to know him, and as exasperating as he often could be, there was something she dearly liked about Manners. After all, for all his foibles, he often tried to do the right thing.

She walked back into her cottage still smiling from the encounter with Manners. Re-entering the kitchen she panicked. It was a smell that immediately assaulted her senses. An unmistakable smell.

SMY STARES DOWN THE BARREL

"I fort 'e was never going to leave."

Smy didn't reply, but stared steadily at a menacingly composed Lydia Lyons. She was sitting at the same table at which Smy and Manners had just been sitting only minutes before.

"What do you want?"

"Nuffin'. Not any more. Not since you walked in frew that door, lady. You and yer mate seem to hol' me in quite 'igh esteem. Yer certainly seem t' know a lot about me."

Lydia Lyons was not only small in height but, Smy suspected, was also what her mother called 'small-boned'. The face was hard but curiously unlined, with eyes that were slightly bulging as if she were in a constant state of surprise. If Smy hadn't already been told by Hoskins that Lyons' age was about forty, she would have estimated her to be easily ten years younger. But the most alarming feature that Lyons bore was a constant slight twitch of her head, which struck Smy as almost like that of a sparrow.

"How long have you been in my house?" Smy spoke steadily, trying to mask the fact that she could feel her heart thumping hard inside her chest.

"Don't get 'oity-toity wiv me, my darlin'. Let's jus' say I took the liberty of waitin' upstairs. Last fing I expected was to see that skinny runt hangin' roun' yer garden. Made me larf listening' to yer both talkin' 'bout my 'arold. Poor 'arold. Wasn't the nicest way to go, but 'e was wery wayward in 'is 'abits."

Smy edged slowly toward the kitchen table. As she did so, Lyons picked up a hessian bag, apparently unaware of Smy's action but then, almost casually, pulled out a revolver. Smy immediately stood still and then began to gradually back away.

"I do love a gun, don't you? An' this one's lovely. Third one I've 'ad. Now what 'appened to the first one, I wonder? Brand new it was when ol' Samuel gave it to me. Must've dropped it somewhere."

"Why did you do that? Why drop the gun in my pocket? Did Spurling suggest that?"

Lyons looked at the revolver as she spoke. "Spurling? Well, it all seemed to be a wery cosy arrangement. Y'see, ol' Laurie Morrie seemed to be fully aware that someone was goin' to kill 'im that night. Tipped off, as it were. Strange enough, 'e even knew who was goin' to do it. Then I find out it was Spurling himself that told Morrie. That's 'ow Morrie knew. So our Mr Morrie 'ad a quiet word wiv Mr Spurling, came to a wery satisfactory financial settlement, an' we all set it up good 'n' proper. I don't know why, but 'e really 'ad it in for you, didn't he? Break 'is 'eart, didja? Whatever you did, 'e saw 'is supposed assassination as the perfect opportunity to settle an' ol' score."

"Did Spurling tell you who wanted Laurie Morrie killed?"

Lyons shrugged. "Not really. And to be honest, I didn't care. When ol' Sam offered me a wery tidy sum for seeing' off some ol' geezer, well, a girl's gotta live, ain't she? I was told 'e'd look like Laurie Morrie and 'e was the one I would shoot. Sammy boy couldn't do it 'imself as 'e was out front wiv the orchestra."

"So you knew all along it wasn't Morrie you'd be killing?"

"I knew it was some guy who'd been creepin' about some poor actress, makin' 'er life a misery. Sam told me 'e was also a nonce. They make me sick, nonces do. It ain't natural doin' what they do. Saw too many of those when I was growin' up."

"So you, Spurling, Morrie and Carver were all in on it together. And I was set up as the killer. And Brighton? That I am not so sure about. My theory is that you knew it was Dowling who killed Spurling and were aware of the link between them. Am I right?"

Lyons stood up and held the gun with both hands, calmly levelling it at Miss Smy's head who was standing only three or four feet away on the opposite side of the kitchen table. "Oh, you are the bright little fing, aren't you, Miss Smy? A wery bright little fing. Yeah, I knew Dowling. I knew what 'e 'ad done."

"You knew Dowling because you were in Spurling's house the day he was killed. Did you see him that day?"

"See 'im? It was me what let 'im in. Then I went upstairs 'cos Spurling wanted me out the way. Said there was summat he needed to talk to the man about in private. First I knew summat was wrong was when I couldn't hear anything downstairs. Nuffin'. Crept down and there 'e was. Laid out wiv a load a' stab wounds all roun' 'is neck. Wasn't pretty. I've seen a few fings in my lifetime but that weren't pretty at all. So I scarpered."

"Dowling knew you were in the house, why didn't he go after you?"

"'Cos I was 'is stooge, weren't I?"

"Stooge? What do you mean?"

Lydia Lyons' arms, tired from holding the revolver up, just

dropped a little with the gun now aimed at Miss Smy's chest. "Stooge. The one that the police were meant to find upstairs and them then finkin' it were me that did ol' Sam in."

"But why go after Dowling?"

Lyons sneered as she spoke. "An' there's me sayin' 'ow bright you were. It's obvious, ain't it? As soon as Dowling knew I wasn't in the picture for Sam's murder, he would 'ave to get me out the way. 'Specially as I knew 'e'd done it. It was going' to 'ave to be 'im or me. So it was 'im."

The terrifying thought dawned on Smy that she was about to be killed in her very own kitchen. With every moment that passed, she was desperately trying to think of some way of saving herself, but her attempts at keeping Lydia Lyons talking seemed to be demanding all of her concentration; there was simply no room for any other thoughts to emerge that might remove the awful peril of her situation.

"So, how did you find out where Dowling was that day in Brighton? All you knew about him was that he was a visitor to Spurling's house."

"The good Lord was on my side, Miss Smy. Y'see, Dowling 'ad killed Mr Spurling before he'd paid me what I was due. Y'know, for killin' that Ventnor geezer. So I thought maybe our Mr Laurie Morrie might see me right. An' I knew where e'd be 'cos Brighton was always a favourite place of mine. An' you'd always see 'im there. An' so 'e was. Walkin' about as bold as brass. Then what do I see next? Only old Dowling pretending to befriend them. Shared a few laughs, they did. Then the three of them went back to Morrie's room."

"But why shoot Morrie and Carver?"

Lyons shrugged her shoulders. "Didn't mean to. I knew they'd ordered room service an' so crept upstairs to Morrie's room. Found this twolley laid up by the staircase and took it wiv me. Knocked and shouted room service but stood with my back to the door, so as to 'ide me face. Morrie opened the door 'n' went back to the table. Didn't bovver lookin'. If 'e 'ad, it might 'ave turned out very different."

"And then you shot Dowling in the back? He never knew it was you who killed him?"

"Yeah. I fink so. It was all a blur at first. Shot Dowlin'. Then saw Morrie get up from the table and then out came Carver from the bathroom. Y'see, I didn't intend to kill 'em all. I needed the money I was owin' but, in the moment and everyfink, I found it was all over before I knew what I'd done. And it was so clear. All so clear. Morrie groaned a bit but 'e didn't take long to go. And Alfred Carver, well 'e died instant e' did."

"Why did you drag Carver's body to the bathroom door?"

"Dunno. Seemed like some sort of plan, but I dunno. 'E weren't as 'eavy as I fort 'e'd be. Anyway, once I'd dragged 'im across the floor, I realised I needed to get outa there quick. I was certain someone must 'ave 'eard the shots so I was out that room quick an' off."

"And, cool as a cucumber, left by the front entrance."

"Can I tell you a secret? Something Mr Spurling told me. When we planned the Framlin'ham shooting, 'e told me to stay calm. Walk slowly and not to make eye contact with anyone. 'E planned it beautifully. An' 'e was right. That day when you came into the dressing room, I dropped that gun in your pocket smooth as you like and no one noticed me."

"And you left the hotel in Brighton in exactly the same way."

Lyons smiled and slowly nodded, as if thrilled by the skill of her murderous art. "And so we met again that day, didn't we,

Miss Smy?"

"Oh yes, we did. And that's why you're here. You knew that I was on to you. And now you have no option but to remove one more witness from the story."

Lyons' outstretched arms raised the gun again towards Smy's head. "That's a wery nice way o' putting it. A bit poetic, I'd say."

"But you won't be able to fire your gun, Lydia. Not with the safety catch on."

Lydia Lyons' arms rested a moment as she glanced at the revolver. That split-second was all that Smy, in her mounting desperation, needed and she pushed the table at Lyons with all of the strength she could muster. The sound of the gun firing was followed by a sprinkling of ceiling plaster showering both women. Smy threw herself across the table and, as she did so, grabbed the teapot which she crashed down onto the skull of her assailant. Lyons was instantly rendered unconscious, tea streaking down her taut, pale skin.

Smy took the revolver and ran outside. To her relief she could see the instantly recognisable frame of Martin Pritty, a local farmhand, emerging from Church Lane. She shouted to him for help and he ran to her cottage and followed her into the house. Lyons was still in the same unconscious state that Smy had left her.

Pritty looked in confusion at the scene, his mouth hanging open as he struggled to find something to say. Eventually, he asked, "What's been goin' on 'ere? Who is she, Fred?"

"Someone who doesn't realise that there is no safety catch on a Webley Mark VI revolver."

ON THE ROAD TO PARHAM

"The Official Secrets Act? Of course I signed it. All policemen have to." Tranmer looked quizzically at Winifred Smy. "Hang on a moment, is what you're about to tell me that important?"

"Yes, it is. Of course, I don't have to tell anyone, but there are times when one carries around something so serious that one feels that the telling of it might give some relief."

It was some time before George Cornish had been able to muster a horse and trap to take Lydia Lyons back to Debenham, where she was incarcerated in one of the two police cells that adjoined the police house on Water Lane. The bruising to her left temple was considerable and she remained confused, at first speaking with little coherence. Smy found herself feeling some sympathy for her, although her rational mind was at a loss as to why her emotional self could be so illogical. After all, wasn't this the woman who was going to occasion the demise of Smy in her own kitchen?

With Lyons safely out of the way, Smy had found herself to be highly agitated. Of course, it wasn't difficult for her to understand why, but the knowledge of all that she had been through seemed to occupy every cell of her body. She was certain that, if she could only communicate the entire experience to someone, it would offer some relief. And that was why she had cycled over to Framlingham and asked for Tranmer at the police station. Thankfully, he was reorganising the files in his office and was glad of the excuse to abandon his task for a walk in the open air.

"This is all to do with the Framlingham murders, I assume?" asked Tranmer.

"It is, and I hope you don't mind. But who else can I talk to?"

"And other than the police, who can you confide in that's also subject to The Official Secrets Act?"

Smy laughed. She knew that, of all the residents in her county, only Tranmer could be completely trusted.

"Hang on a minute," continued Tranmer. "Have you signed the act as well? If not, I'm not sure it's wise to continue."

"I have, but don't ask me when. I signed the 1889 act, not the 1911 one you would have been presented with."

"You? Why would…"

Smy stopped and looked warmly at Tranmer, not speaking for a moment whilst she considered her response. "Herbert, shall we take the Parham road? It's been a while since I've walked along it."

Although the early morning had been chilly, the emerging sun had cleared away the heavier cloud and there was a pleasant warmth in the soft wind. Smy noticed, with some sadness, that the snowy umbels of the delicate cow parsley had now disappeared, a sign that spring was now making way for the summer to follow.

"I do not want to sensationalise what I am about to tell you, but what I shall communicate is known to a very few. Some of those few that do know sit at the very heart of Government and, therefore, I am placing myself in a vulnerable situation. Of course, If Mr Manners…"

"There's no need to warn me. We will have our conversation today and then no more will be said about it, either between us or anyone else. You have my word."

'Then I need to begin with how I met Laurie Morrie. When I first went to London I knew no one, but soon became acquainted with a nice woman called Eleanor Wright who introduced me to her brother, Lawrence. He was already working in music halls, although at the time he was a very minor act. Quite 'bottom-of-the-bill', as they say. For reasons I would rather not explain, he took against me and made accusations which were untrue and hurtful. There are two things you quickly come to realise about Lawrence Wright: the first is that he always had an unhealthy relationship with gambling; the second is that he was a man who carried his resentments with an intensity that bordered on the obsessive."

"And yet when you see him perform…"

"Exactly. You would not realise that beneath that sunny exterior is a very complicated man."

Tranmer found a long branch at the side of the road which he inspected and started to brush against the wild grasses on the verge. "Often the case, I believe. I hear the same thing said about comics."

"Quite so. Anyway, not long after Eleanor and I became very good friends, I found employment with Lord Kenilworth as a governess. He was a man with many links in Europe and, when visiting Germany as part of his household, I was asked to undertake a small errand. It was nothing really, but it did mean that I was required to sign the Official Secrets Act and be introduced to a senior figure in the Secret Service Bureau. You will find this history germane to all that has happened recently."

Tranmer could not hide his shock at this revelation. "Secret Service? I don't know what to say. Sounds like it was more than a small errand, Winifred."

"It really was all very minor, and I don't want to dwell on what I did. It has nothing to do with what I am relating to you now."

Bored with thrashing the grasses, Tranmer bore the stick on his shoulder, as if it was a rifle and he part of some regimental parade. "Every time I think I know you, you surprise me with some new revelation. You are such an enigma, my friend."

"I am no enigma, believe me. I am not at all interesting. But we are getting sidetracked and I must continue."

Tranmer gave a mock salute as a gesture of agreement.

"So, in late April, what do I discover? That the now-famous Laurie Morrie is appearing at Framlingham and a letter arrives from his assistant, Alfred Carver, communicating that Morrie would like to see me. I reason that, perhaps, time has diminished some of the more unpleasant aspects of his character and that it might bury a rather old hatchet. Morrie then sends me free tickets to the first and - as it transpired - only night's performance, and I decide that I would go. On the night, both Gladys Cupper and I meet him and he seems perfectly polite. No mention is made of our having once fallen out and Gladys and I proceed to watch the show that night. The debacle that followed is too well known to you for me to have to repeat it, but I suddenly found myself accused of Laurie Morrie's murder and being harangued by Inspector Sibley to supply a full confession."

Tranmer, now tired of the gun-stick, threw it into the hedge. "Yes, Sibley did have the bit between his teeth on that. But you have to admit the circumstances…"

"I would not argue with the initial impression I might have given, but one hopes that one's character would have some degree of validity."

"It was the gun that had been planted on you that raised the first doubt, if I remember right?"

"It was and I will return to the gun presently. Next, once I was released, I find out that Laurie Morrie and Alfred Carver had disappeared. I also learned that, despite there being two performances, they had only booked one night in The Crown Hotel. This confirmed my suspicion that they had no intention of staying in Framlingham for a second evening."

"So they both knew what was going to happen? The shooting and everything."

"Absolutely. Reserving accommodation for only one night was their first error; the second was the invitation I received to go to London and meet a Miss Marguerite de Gruchy at the Goring Hotel."

With no stick to now occupy him, Tranmer decided to put his hands into his pockets. "Now I am totally in the dark. All that happened in Framlingham, the two deaths and everything, we have already spoken about in the past. But what happened once you went off on your travels is a complete blank for me. This Marguerite de Gruchy. Who exactly was she?"

"It's funny you ask that because, as I'm explaining myself to you, things begin to strike me. There were three people who were not who I thought they were. The first was Laurie Morrie, slumped across the dressing room table after he'd been shot. Eventually we find out it wasn't him, but poor Horace Ventnor. The second was Marguerite de Gruchy, whom I quickly knew to be fake. That was someone called Polly Armscott. And the third we will come to in time."

With the temperature of the day slowly rising, Smy took off her hat and started to fan herself with it. Tranmer removed his hat as well and held it by his thigh, turning it every so often between his thumb and middle finger.

"So why the whole charade with Marguerite de Gruchy? I remember you telling me about the napkin and everything. What was the point of that?"

"Oh, that was easy enough to work out. I think that once Lawrence had learned of my release, he would have been desperate to know how much I knew and who I might be talking to. Creating a character like Miss de Gruchy was a first attempt to gain my confidence. But it was such a poor deception, pretending to be his fiancée was just one mistake. Besides, unless he'd drastically changed his taste in women since I'd first met him, our Miss de Gruchy would never have been his type."

"Do you know what I don't understand? I don't understand why he would go to all the trouble of exacting his revenge in such a roundabout way. And the setup he used, it was all so elaborate. Enlighten me if you can, because I'm completely at a loss, Winifred."

"That was where I was wrong and it was some time before I began to see what was truly unfolding in front of me. Herbert, my being framed for Ventnor's murder was a convenient by-product of something far bigger. Something so important that both Sibley and Manners were immediately told to forget the two murders."

"When you told me earlier that Lawrence had a gambling problem, well that all made sense. I thought that someone he owed money to wanted him dead and thought some out-of-the-way small town would be the perfect place to do it. But they shot the wrong man, and eventually caught up with him again in Brighton. No mistakes made a second time. Gambling is full of undesirable characters, as I know only too well from doing this job."

"I predict that what you have just said will become the official interpretation of those events. It will stop tongues wagging and everyone will be satisfied and able to go about their business again. And Spurling's death will likewise be explained away. But the truth is much, much darker than that. Herbert, Lawrence Wright wasn't killed because he owed people money."

"So why did someone want him killed?"

"They wanted him killed because he was betraying his country."

BETRAYAL

The expression on Tranmer's face changed continually as he tried to take in what Smy had just said.

"I…I find that hard to believe. He's…well, he's so well-known."

"Espionage is somehow beneath the calling of a music hall star, perhaps?"

"Well, no. Well, yes. I can't quite believe what you've just told me. How? How could someone who is so much in the public eye get away with that?"

Smy glanced around, but the farmer who was leading his pony and trap was still too far away to have heard their conversation. They walked on in silence for a while and, when she was sure that they were alone again, she continued with how she had tried to meet up with the elusive Polly Armscott, the contact that Miss de Gruchy had told her about. How a man had followed Polly through the underground to her house whom Smy, in turn, had also tried to follow. She then related the circumstances of her first contact with Dowling and the fact that he knew exactly who Smy was, even down to her own activities, many years ago, in the SSB.

"And then you went to Brighton?"

"That was where I encountered the third person pretending

to be someone else. I stayed at a small guesthouse. There were several guests staying there but two stood out. A serious-minded, quiet army officer called Joyce and another resident who was an odious salesman, quite taken with the sound of his own voice."

"What was his name?"

"Todd." Smy smiled to herself as she recalled his antics that one morning at breakfast. "But that wasn't his real name. He was a colleague of Dowling and knew that our seemingly pillar-of-the-community army officer was a link in a long chain through which vital and secret information was passing. Someone, probably Lawrence, had tipped Joyce off about me and, if it hadn't been for our awful Mr Todd, Joyce would have been my nemesis."

Tranmer was now in deep thought, with his head bowed as he stared at the ground. "No, I still don't see where Lawrence, or Laurie, or whatever-his-name-is, fits in. I think I'm a bit lost."

"The SSB had already received information that the German army had anticipated two supposedly highly secret surprise raids. Now they knew that there must be a leak in the chain of command somewhere as very few people knew that the raids were to take place. So a careful trap was laid by creating information about a supposed army offensive to recapture ground lost in the Ypres salient."

"And they found their man?"

"No, they found their woman: Polly Armscott. She worked at the heart of the Admiralty and, in her position, was typing highly secret orders and memos that very few had access to. Luckily, someone at the Admiralty found Polly secreting a carbon of one such letter in her coat and had passed on her suspicions to her superiors. She was the first link in the chain."

"My god. I take it that she then communicated the plan to Wright?"

"Wright was in a bad way financially. When I first knew him, whatever he lost through horses and whatever, he would always be able to win back at cards. But fortune had obviously changed for Lawrence Wright and now whatever he won at cards, he lost three times over on other gambling addictions. Look closely enough and you'll soon find unregulated gambling dens all over London. As you said earlier, the people who frequent them are not mixing with polite company, and when someone as well-known as Laurie Morrie falls heavily into debt, the vultures soon descend on their prey."

"So someone recruited him to the German side?"

"They did. And the operation ran smoothly for many months until Polly Armscott was rumbled. She was never Lawrence's fiancée, but Alfred Carver's. Knowing that there was espionage activity in Brighton, and that Polly was leaking these same secrets, it didn't take them long to find the link between the two. Wright had such a hold over Carver that he persuaded Polly to pass what she could to him; he would then take the information and meet up with a contact in Brighton, who we now know to have been our Mr Joyce."

Herbert Tranmer asked Smy to stop at that point, conscious that he was beginning to lose his way again in all the detail. "And where did you say this Joyce man was based? In Brighton?"

"No, he had accommodation in Hove, but he worked at Newhaven, just along the coast. As you know, Newhaven is a key supply point for the armies fighting on the Western Front. Joyce had access not only to information about British strategy, but even the stores housing the ammunition, clothing and so on. The Secret Service Bureau had been watching Joyce and Armscott for some time, trying to see where the final link was: how did they get the information across to the Germans? And that will be difficult to establish now that Joyce is dead."

They both continued their walk, Smy feeling something lift from her shoulders now that she had told Tranmer. The call of an olive-brown chiffchaff was carried along by the wind, its repetitive staccato notes hurrying in an orderly, fast-moving queue. A scrambling noise was heard from the depth of the ditch, Smy's attuned ear instantly recognising the hidden, fevered running of a rabbit.

"This is all quite some story. But what about Framlingham? I can't see where that fits in with what you've told me."

Smy drew in a sharp breath. "This is where I will most need your discretion, Herbert. We share so much in common. We value many of the same things. What I am about to tell you are actions that the population of this country would be astonished to learn."

Herbert Tranmer rubbed his hand across his chin. "Well, you've told me enough already so I don't think we can stop now."

"Once the SSB realised that they still didn't know what the last link was, how the information was reaching the central powers in Germany, Austria, and Hungary, and the fact that there may be others who might be supplying information to Joyce, they had to act. So they decided to make a decision about breaking the chain once and for all. Their first decision, and I'm sure that Joyce would have been next, was to eliminate Lawrence Wright."

"Kill Wright? It was the Government's own secret service

that ordered his murder?"

"As I said, Herbert, many would be astonished to know what I've just told you."

Tranmer's hand was now rubbing the back of his neck, as he reeled from the shock of Smy's intelligence. "But if they planned to kill Lawrence Wright, surely Polly Armscott would have known about it? After all, she was on the inside of things."

Smy shook her head. "No, the Secret Service Bureau was quite independent of the Admiralty. Polly Armscott would never have known about such a decision. Anyway, by this time they knew that Polly Armscott wasn't to be trusted and so went straight to the person who was to arrange Wright's killing. And this might be the next shock for you."

A rueful smile was instantly noticeable on Tranmer's face. "I'm beginning to think that I might be immune to any further shocks, even if you told me it was the Archbishop of Canterbury. Do I know who they wanted to kill Wright?"

"You know his chosen assassin very well. It was Samuel Spurling."

ALL THE PIECES FIT

"But Spurling was murdered as well? And he was just…just a…"

"What do you know of Spurling?"

"Know of him? He was some sort of music teacher. Everyone knows about him. Winifred, are you sure about this?"

"Maybe you'd have believed me if I'd said the Archbishop of Canterbury, after all?"

But Tranmer had chosen to stare across the fields, feeling the need to divert his attention whilst his mind absorbed this unsettling information. "Why would they ask someone like Spurling? Besides, wasn't he supposed to be conducting that small orchestra that night? He would have been too obvious."

"Spurling worked with Dowling, many years before, but had proven unreliable, especially when it came to drink. Apparently, in his heyday, he was a formidable intellect and physically very strong, but the alcohol had taken a heavy toll and he was eventually retired to a far-off little town, out of harm's way."

"You mean Framlingham?"

"Exactly. But he was retired on the proviso that, to collect a small retainer from the government, he might still be called upon to carry out the occasional assignment. As

213

Dowling already had his hands full with Polly Armscott and the Brighton link, he delegated the removal of Laurie Morrie to Spurling. It was Dowling's idea to arrange the whole charity concert, so as to place Lawrence Wright within easy reach of Spurling. Spurling had been told to be discreet and to make it look like he'd been shot by a spurned lover. But that's where things went askew."

"Hang on, was it Spurling who tipped off Wright about the plan? Why would he do that?"

"Simple. Because he'd spotted another opportunity to make some money. I believe that Spurling mistakenly thought that Laurie Morrie was a rich man, and so had approached him with an offer that would benefit Spurling financially, and spare Morrie his life."

"Pay off the assassin, you mean?"

"Exactly. I'm sure that Morrie's quick thinking and charm would have convinced Spurling that the money would be found. And it even gave Morrie the perfect opportunity to settle an old score with me. If all went well, then not only would Morrie escape with his life, but he could also make things very uncomfortable for me."

"So the whole deception was planned by Spurling and Morrie?"

"Carver must have been involved as well. He must have nominated Ventnor to take Morrie's place which would then dispose of the inconvenience of having his poor Polly plagued by a misfit. Before the concert, both Morrie and Carver were the apogee of friendliness to me, which made me immediately suspicious."

Tranmer stopped walking once more and looked around. "You know, I think we might need to head back. But Spurling?

I can't believe…hang on, but it was this Lyons woman who killed Ventnor, not Spurling."

"You will recall the time when we went to the rear of the Assembly Hall, and I pointed out to you that the door into the main dressing room had recently been bricked up. Spurling was quite devious, because I could never understand how Lydia Lyons got inside the dressing room without being seen by Ventnor. Spurling lent a wardrobe to the charity show that evening which, when I was with Spurling's dead body waiting for you to return from the police station, I had the luxury of examining. What I noticed instantly was that one of the two back panels had clearly been removed and replaced; the nails were different to the other panel that had been left untouched."

"Yes, I do remember you suggesting to me that Sibley might want to take a close look at the wardrobe. So, after Ventnor had been persuaded to take Wright's position at the dressing table, Morrie must have left telling the unfortunate stand-in that Polly Armscott - the bait he had set for Ventnor - would come into the room at any moment?"

"Exactly. But it was Lyons who entered, quietly coming in through the back door of the room, through the wardrobe and…no more Ventnor. You'll remember that I had been asked to go to the dressing room and, well, let's just say the timing of the whole operation was perfect. She waited for me to give the distinctive knock, then must have emerged from the wardrobe and shot Ventnor. I burst in and Lyons plants the gun on me with all the skill of a veteran pickpocket."

"And Spurling had his alibi as he was still with the orchestra?"

"He was. There was no blood on his hands at all that night, but there were machinations definitely on his mind."

"Machinations?"

"Apparently, he saw an opportunity to secure a financial favour from the Secret Service Bureau for his silence about the whole operation. After all, with a country at war, the ruthless slaying of an innocent man who was originally thought to be a much-loved music hall star would make for some rather uncomfortable headlines."

"He was trying to blackmail the Secret Service?"

"Well, perhaps trying to persuade them that he was worth more than the rather meagre stipend he was already receiving. He also claimed that he needed to pay the real killer off and was short of money to do that. Of course, having arranged Wright's killing in exactly the opposite way to how the SSB wanted it executed was irritating enough. But for Spurling to then take matters into his own hands and come to a cosy arrangement with Wright - and try and dupe the SSB into a financial reward for his inventiveness - was a step too far. What with that and the threat that the whole operation might be exposed, the SSB were left with only one choice."

"Was it your man Dowling?"

"It was the nature of Spurling's killing that first alerted me. When most people have been run through with a knife they do not die instantly. I will spare you the anatomical reasons, but for many who have been stabbed, the process of dying can be drawn out and very painful."

"How do you know this?"

"Oh, believe me, Herbert, I know. What did the post-mortem tell you about the way Spurling had been killed?"

Tranmer thought for a moment as he tried to recall the report. "Let's see, it was an upward stab wound to the back of the neck I think. Whatever it was, the brainstem…"

"…would have been severed instantly. Hardly the technique

of your average killer. Death would have been instant. The body we saw that day had been dispatched by a professional. Yes, to now answer your question, it was Dowling. And whilst he stealthily carried out his gory assignment, Lydia Lyons was upstairs in the house all the time."

"But why kill Wright and Carver and Dowling? Surely she would have wanted to keep a very low profile. Not go searching for people."

"I can't be certain and there are some things we may never know, but my instincts point me towards Joyce. He may well have cottoned on to the fact that the chain had been uncovered. Perhaps Wright or Carver contacted him directly to tell him the game was up, even passing on the name of Lydia Lyons as Spurling's proxy for the killing. There's also the fact that it would have been to Lyons' advantage to have Wright and Carver out of the way. They could easily tell the authorities that she was the murderer of Spurling to divert attention. Whatever it was, she dealt with them both and exacted revenge on Dowling at the same time."

Smy and Tranmer walked at an ambling pace past the train station. Outwardly, they looked like two friends taking the air, perhaps exchanging the occasional piece of gossip as friends do. After all, who was to know that they had just shared information that would have shocked a country already growing weary of the war's relentless slaughter?

"So, Winifred, we started with Lydia Lyons. And we end with Lydia Lyons. She had you firmly in her sights as well."

"I feared she might. That's twice I have stared death in the face in the last week or so. I don't want it to be third time unlucky. Anyway, let's turn our minds to more wholesome matters. How is Miss Clemence?"

Tranmer began to jangle some coins in his pocket and pursed his lips as if ruminating about how to answer. "She's fine, I suppose."

"I suppose? That's a strange response."

"Well, if I am to be absolutely honest, I've found her manner rather distant. Ever since she told me about the brief exchange you had with her after coming to see me at the police station."

At that moment, Smy found herself feeling rather ashamed and triumphant in equal measure.

GOD IS IN HIS HEAVEN

Three weeks had passed since her long conversation with Tranmer; Smy had not heard from him since and she now occupied herself tending the vegetables in her garden. Fledglings were already beginning their great struggle to survive and the warmer days had caused the verges around Kenton to erupt in a cascade of grasses and wildflowers.

She realised that she still had to return two books to Mrs Chevallier at Aspall Hall, so decided to do so after calling into Debenham to buy some white cotton so that she could do a few repairs on various garments. She had only cycled as far as the vicarage when she was met by the Reverend Pilbeam, who was walking towards the church.

"A very beautiful day, is it not, Miss Smy? *The lark's on the wing; the snail's on the thorn: god's in his heaven - all's right with the world!*"

"Browning?"

"Browning, indeed. Your education has not been wasted. *Pippa Passes.* Or perhaps that should be Miss Smy passes? *Quo vadis, Miss Smy?*"

"Oh, just off to Debenham to pick up a couple of things and then calling in at Aspall Hall. And you Mr Pilbeam?"

"A pastoral visit to Oak Farm. By the way, that was a nasty

business with that woman. I don't know the details but you obviously had an enemy there, my dear. Percy Whiting thought her very odd."

"Oh, it was nothing. I'd rather forget about it now. I might see you on Sunday."

"God is a commitment, Miss Smy. Not an occasional pleasure. Do come."

Winifred Smy made her excuses and continued on to Bellwell Lane. Pilbeam's reference to the encounter with Lydia Lyons set her thinking about the fact that she has been confronted twice by the same type of revolver. In trying to untangle all the myriad threads of the last few weeks, the significance of the Webley revolver had escaped her.

Thinking it over as she breezed between the verges resplendent with campion and hogweed, she teased out that there would have been the same type of revolver present at four significant events. The first would have been the killing of Ventnor. It was easy to surmise that the gun had been supplied by Dowling, although he was expecting it to be used by Spurling, not Lydia Lyons. The second occasion was the shooting of the three men in Brighton. That gun would probably have been procured by Joyce and passed on to Lydia Lyons.

Joyce had carried the same make and model of revolver the night that he had followed Miss Smy. It would have been a bullet from that gun that would have ushered her into the next world if it hadn't been for Hoskins' timely intervention.

And then, finally, she found herself staring down its barrel when Lydia Lyons had cornered her in her own kitchen. Yes, she concluded, if she never saw a Webley Mark VI revolver again, it would be a blessing for her.

She made first for the draper's shop, the long side-wall of which flanked one bank of the River Deben. She was greeted by Becky Lummis, a young woman whom Miss Smy had little time for, having an opinion of her own importance and intelligence that was singularly of an inverse proportion to those factors.

"Could you show me the different cotton reels you have?"

But before the counter assistant could reply, there was a tremendous crash from behind as the door was flung aside, followed by the entrance of a furiously upset Edith Gladwell.

"That's what your white feather does to families, you…" But there the sentence died as, overcome with grief, she could no longer speak, but instead slammed down a sheet of paper on the glass counter with such force that Smy thought it a miracle that it didn't shatter. Edith Gladwell left as violently as she entered, leaving behind her an awful silence as both Smy and Miss Lummis tried to comprehend what had just happened.

Becky Lummis's right hand, which had automatically been held by her chest when confronted by Mrs Gladwell, now picked up the letter and unfolded it. She said nothing but instead, with shaking hands, placed it down again and walked through a curtain that separated the front from the back of the draper's shop.

Smy, feeling it something of an impertinence but unable to deny herself, picked up the letter. It was from a Captain R. Sebastian-Haigh.

My dear Mr and Mrs Gladwell

I regret very much to inform you that your son Pte. William Gladwell, No. 18679 of this Company was killed in action on the morning of the 10th instant. Death was instantaneous and without any suffering.

The Company was taking part in an attack and your son's gun team was one of those which advanced against the enemy. The attack was successful, and all guns reached and established new positions. Later in the afternoon, the enemy shelled our lines and one shell fell on your son's gun killing him and wounding a comrade.

It was impossible to get his remains away and he lies in a soldier's grave where he fell.

I and the Commanding Officer and all the Company deeply sympathise with you in your loss.

Your son always did his duty and now has given his life for his country. We all honour him, and I trust you will feel some consolation in remembering this.

His effects will reach you via the base in due course.

With deepest sympathy to you both.

Captain R. Sebastian-Haigh

Smy folded the letter up and put it into her bag in case Edith Gladwell might wish it to be returned. She put aside all thoughts of cotton and sewing repairs and walked outside into the warmth of the May morning. She glanced up and down the High Street to see if Mrs Gladwell was still in the vicinity, but looked in vain. In this small corner of Suffolk, life was continuing as normal. Slaughter and war had been unleashed in another universe, but not here. It was a realisation that perhaps, thought Smy, bordered on the obscene.

"Oh yes, god might be in his heaven, reverend, but there is nothing right in the world."

Acknowledgments

Once more, I would like to thank those who have generously contributed to this book. I must first thank my wife, Penny, for all her valuable advice and suggestions, constant encouragement and immaculate proofreading. I would also like to extend my appreciation to Maud Henry for correcting my schoolboy French and to John Bridges at the Lanman Museum, Framlingham, for answering my queries.

The wonderful cover design is, once again, provided by Lucy Johnson, and I repeat my indebtedness to Doreen and David Matthews for all of the lovely conversations we have had over the last few years on 'all things Suffolk'. Last of all, I would wish to acknowledge the considerable research undertaken by Elizabeth Barrett, which I have constantly drawn on when writing about Kenton: the church, village and environs

Melissa Nash has created an excellent period map of the Kenton district to complement both this book and the previous three novellas in the Winifred Smy series. It is free to download from the link below:

https://michaelheathauthor.com/genres/murder-mystery